D1114863

Three Loves Has Sandy

THREE LOVES HAS SANDY

by Amelia Elizabeth Walden

Whittlesey House

McGraw-Hill Book Company, Inc.

NEW YORK TORONTO LONDON

Also by Amelia Elizabeth Walden

GATEWAY

WAVERLY

SUNNYCOVE

SKYMOUNTAIN

MARSHA ON-STAGE

VICTORY FOR JILL

A GIRL CALLED HANK

ALL MY LOVE

DAYSTAR

THIRD PRINTING

This book has appeared serially in "The American Girl."

Library of Congress Catalog Card Number: 55-8294

Published by Whittlesey House
A division of the McGraw-Hill Book Company, Inc.
Printed in the United States of America

Three Loves Has Sandy

1

WHEN Sandy crossed the long stretch of football field that lay between the school and the softball diamond, she saw him.

"There he is," she said to Dodo Frazer, the team's catcher, who had come out early to help Sandy warm up her pitching arm. "The biggest pest in town—Wyoming Bill."

He sat back on his heels, cowboy fashion, in the first row of the bleachers, the sole spectator at girls' softball practice. His broadbrimmed Stetson was pushed back, revealing a thatch of blond curly hair bleached to the color of lemon peel. He had been attending New Sharon High School for exactly two weeks and already he was a prominent character in the school, a V.I.P. The first day he had sauntered through the halls in his colorful outfit, checked shirt, frontier pants, and ponyskin belt, and those flamboyant red cowboy boots that clicked like any girl's high heels, the school crowd had taken to him, dubbing him Vaquero or Tumbleweed or Wyoming Bill.

The Wyoming Bill had stuck, and even Sandy grudgingly admitted it was an apt nickname. He looked like Wyoming, all six feet of him. It was not the clothes so much as the stance, the attitude toward life. Expansive was the word for it. From the tip of his yellow hair down through the blinding blue eyes, the crooked smile, the large nose, the sprinkling of generous-sized freckles over a turf-tan skin, down the whole lean, muscular length of this boy, there was not a cramped or petty quality anywhere.

Sandy glanced over at him now, sitting there with typical Western nonchalance. He was spinning two ropes, one in each hand, but he managed to smile and wave to her.

"Show-off," she mumbled to Dodo. "Always following me. Everywhere I go. Last night and the night before, he came down to the sandlot and barged in while I was coaching the Blue Devils and the Supermen. Had to show them that he knows a lot more about softball than anyone here in the East. Him and his windmill windup! I wish he'd wind himself up so tight he'd disappear."

"I thought no one but the team was allowed at softball practices," Dodo said. "Miss MacDonald's orders."

"Sure, but he's found some gimmick for worming his way in. The way he does with everyone. Probably offered to keep score or umpire or maybe even coach the B team. That's the way he is, always got some angle of getting in everywhere."

Sandy did not elaborate, but she might have. All the time she kept winding up and putting them across the plate to Dodo, she kept thinking about Wyoming Bill. She would not have dared to tell Dodo the half of it. It would be all over the school, the way he had been hounding her this past week, and the last thing she wanted was to become known as Wyoming Bill's—or anyone else's, for that matter!—girl.

It was just her luck that this tall Westerner had moved in with his aunt and uncle, the Peabodys, right on Sandy's own bailiwick, Gardner Street. The neighbors gossiped about him, the way they did about everyone, saying he had come East when his father's ranch had been burned out. Rumor had it that Wyoming Bill and his family were locking horns over his schooling. His parents wanted him to go to his grandfather's and great-grandfather's college in the East next year. Bill held out for a Western school. So his parents had offered him this few months' trial period in New England while their ranch was being rebuilt. If Bill liked it, he stayed. If he didn't, he went back.

When Sandy thought of the way he had disrupted her life these past few days, she wished some miracle would happen to carry him back West tomorrow—preferably by a nonstop airplane. Yesterday he had not been satisfied with taking the sandlot coaching of the two kid teams out of her hands and showing off that wonderful windmill windup of his.

Oh no, that wasn't enough. He had to insist on walking her home just before supper and getting himself introduced to her family. Last night, more than ever before, Sandy wished for a mother to talk things over with. A mother would have interceded. A mother might have understood why Sandy didn't want to be bothered with this long drink of water out of the West.

Marlene, her much older sister who had, in many ways, done a good job of pinch-hitting for the Herzog children's mother, was no help where Wyoming Bill was concerned. She was too easily flattered, and Bill was lavish with his compliments. He even got himself invited to supper. Listening to him praise Marlene's warmed-over pot roast and strawberry shortcake, and admire her older brother Greg for his job as reporter on the *New Sharon News* and then offer to spend an entire evening with her other brother, Ran, and his ham radio station, Sandy found herself building up a terrific resistance to this charmer in the checked shirt and blue pants and red boots.

Although his special kind of enthusiasm rubbed her the wrong way, she had to admit he had plenty of know-how. He wasn't just sounding off when he showed interest in Greg's politics and Ran's radio set. He talked their language, just the way he talked the language of the kids down on the sandlot. His windmill windup *was* good. Even Sandy had been left breathless as she watched him swing his right arm forward and up, then backward and down. Up and down. Up and down. Sandy almost died of suspense wondering on which swing of the arm he would release the ball. Then when he had delivered it, it was a terrifically fast ball, so fast that she had let out an envious whistle and exclaimed, "What a pitch! What a beautiful, beautiful pitch!"

But she wasn't going to be won over by a softball pitch, no matter how beautiful it was. She had a pretty good one of her own, and while it was not the fabulous windmill that had come out of the West like a tornado, it was an excellent figure-eight or "pretzel" windup and last year it had made her team the champions of the county, and unless she broke her arm or sprained her wrist, she expected to do equally well this year.

With a little effort, Sandy put Wyoming Bill out of her thoughts and gave her attention to the job at hand. After all, he was only a boy, but her business this afternoon was pitching. Out here she was monarch of all she surveyed. This was her territory. Although the team had not elected her captain this year—a disappointment she had found rather hard to take—she was the undisputed leader of the team. Wendy Mason, the captain, was a figurehead. She dabbled in sports the way she dabbled in many other activities: dramatics, cheerleading, dancing, dating. The girls admired Wendy for her sophistication, but when it came to rallying for a victory, it was Sandy they turned to.

Sandy was a good pitcher and she knew it. She worked hard at it. She had a lot of natural stuff in her favor—a first-rate arm, a good eye, a way with a ball, imperturbable poise on the pitcher's plate, not a nerve in her body, the stamina of an ox.

She did only one thing that Miss MacDonald was always shaking her head over, always cautioning her about. She let her temper fly on the pitcher's plate. "Don't be so hotheaded," her teammates would say to her. "Someday your temper is going to make trouble for us."

This year she was a sophomore. That made her important in every way. The difficult adjustments of the freshman year were behind her. She was at home in high school. She knew the kids and the teachers. She had found her niche as Sandy Herzog. They accepted her for what she was, a roly-poly fun-loving girl who would dress and act and talk as she wished, bright enough in her classes, not interested in boys, liking two things more than anything else in the world—softball and horses.

This afternoon her pitching arm felt good. She knew how to take care of it, knew enough not to throw too hard early in the season while the muscles were tender. If her arm felt tired she never practiced pitching against the old mattress Greg had hung up for her against their garage door at home. Today the weight of the ball was light, so she knew her arm was in the pink. She would warm up just a little, taking no risks of tiring herself out before the practice game began.

"All right, girls, let's go." It was Miss MacDonald's usual signal to play ball. The stragglers took their positions. The members of the B team lined up for their turn at bat. Sandy glanced over the field to be sure all her own teammates were on the job. She placed her feet squarely on the pitcher's plate and held the ball in both hands about a foot in front of her body, with her elbows lightly touching her sides.

There was that momentary hush over the field as the girls waited for her pitch. This was her moment. Dodo Frazer squatted near the batter. Dodo was a small, slight girl with a solemn expression that earned for her various grim nicknames like "Gloom-puss" and "Weepy" and "Tear-jerker." Her deadpan expression was a great asset in her position as catcher and she was a clever one at sizing up every batter psychologically, then slyly giving out her signals for the pitch.

Tall Cynthia Gibbs was at bat. Dodo signaled that the target would be a low one, because Cynthia tended to swing high. Sandy got the signal and started the delivery by turning her body to the right.

She was aware of Miss MacDonald's voice shouting instructions to the players of both teams. This was the way Miss MacDonald coached. She would sit on the bench near the diamond and shout her instructions to members of both varsity and B teams: the pitcher, the catcher, the first and third basemen, the shortstop, the outfielders, and especially the girl at bat. The continual flow of instructions never eased. The girls were used to it.

Sandy delivered the ball and it passed straight over the home plate just above Cynthia's knees. She did not attempt to hit it, and Ellie Winchester, team manager and acting umpire, called, "Strike!"

Cynthia showed signs of nervousness. The whole B team were petrified when they came to bat against Sandy because they never knew what she would do next. Her grimaces, her shiftiness on the plate, the variety of her pitches kept them on the defensive. In the interschool games she had tougher competition, but here in practice games she went to town, enjoying herself to the hilt as she struck out one batter after another.

They went through three innings like this, with the B team being struck out as fast as they took the bat and the varsity running up an impressive number of runs.

As Sandy walked toward the pitcher's plate at top of

the fourth inning, she was aware of Miss MacDonald standing in a huddle with the players from the B team. She was surprised to see Wyoming Bill in there too, talking with the coach and the girls. Miss MacDonald was laughing—she was one of those rare teachers with a sense of humor—and Sandy would have given two inches off her pitching arm to know what they were talking about.

"All set, girls," Miss MacDonald called as the B team took their places and Ellie Winchester gave the signal to play ball.

Sandy grounded her feet solidly on the pitcher's plate, getting ready for her delivery and all the while watching Mabel Gratz at the bat. Mabel was short and dumpy, almost as broad as she was wide, but she could pack a mean wallop at the bat if you gave her half a chance. She was the one player on the B team who was not afraid of Sandy, openly boasting of this, saying that no comic-sheet with a fast ball could rattle her. However, Sandy knew her weakness. Mabel could be tempted to swing at high and low balls which were not strikes. She was a fool for a bad pitch, unable to resist the temptation to swing at it.

Dodo signaled to Sandy to pitch close to the belt and low.

Sandy went into her windup, swinging her arm and grimacing at the belligerent Mabel, who glared back defiantly at her.

Then, as Sandy released the ball, she became aware of a strange sound piercing the air. A voice with an unmistakable drawl was bellowing at Mabel, "Gratzy, don't swing!"

The ball was low, a bad pitch, intentionally so because both Dodo and Sandy had been sure Mabel would be tempted to swing. Mabel, however, heeded the voice from the stands and did not swing.

"Ball one," Ellie Winchester called.

Sandy would not deign to glance over to the stands from which the interference had come. She guessed she knew Wyoming Bill's voice by now.

She tried again, this time heeding Dodo's signal to pitch to an inside target because Mabel was hugging and crowding the plate. Sandy wound up. She went through the most intricate legal windup in her repertory.

Then, just as she was about to deliver the ball, that voice sailed out from the stands. "Don't pay any attention to her contortions, Gratzy. Keep your eye on the ball!"

The pitch was a good one this time and Mabel Gratz swung at it, meeting it squarely and whamming it clear into the middle of next week. She ran to first, to second, to third, and then to home base with the cheers and screams of the B team following her and high above them all the friendly bellow of the Tornado from Wyoming, shouting, "Go it, Gratzy. Go it. You can make home. Atta girl!"

He kept it up throughout the rest of the game. Whenever Sandy pitched, the voice of Wyoming Bill was like the voice of doom from the stands, coaching the B team with a shrewdness that would have been astounding if it were not so maddening.

Sandy was hot. She was hot and furious. She tore off her neckerchief, then her sweatshirt. Then she opened the neck of her striped linen shirt. She did not lose her poise on the plate and she did not stop pitching. She kept at it, matching that cowboy-on-the-loose with a pitch for every one of his instructions, coming back again and again. She did not get rattled, but she did get mad and she wished for two minutes after he had made her throw three balls in a row that she had a water pistol instead of a ball in her hand. She would have enjoyed aiming straight for that bronco buster in the bleachers.

The practice broke up with the B team having scored five runs, an unprecedented number for a practice game. Every one of those runs had been the result of Wyoming Bill's coaching.

Sandy shouted her head off about it all the way home. Dodo gave her a lift, along with Ellie Winchester and Pat Manero, who played shortstop. Sandy told them she couldn't understand how Miss MacDonald could permit such interference. Why, that cowboy had taken the practice right out of the coach's hands!

The girls were sympathetic. They thought Wyoming Bill had a terrible nerve, but in a way you had to admit he was amusing. Clever, too. His instructions to the B team had worked. As for Miss MacDonald, well, you know how she was. Broad-minded and tolerant. It wasn't the first time she had let someone help coach. Especially if that someone knew anything about the game, and you had to admit this cowboy knew a lot about softball.

With such cold comfort as she got from her teammates, Sandy stopped talking and brooded in silence. She was still brooding after supper when Marlene called upstairs that someone wanted to see her.

"Who?" she shouted downstairs. It could be Dodo or Ellie with a homework problem.

"Come down and see," Marlene answered.

So she did. It was Wyoming Bill, all six feet of him, filling the big kitchen with his geniality.

"Hi," he said. Marlene looked from Bill to Sandy and then made a great show of having some sewing to do upstairs. When they were alone, which was the last thing in the world Sandy wanted, he said, "I've come to say I'm sorry. I think you got mad at me this afternoon."

"Why should I get mad?" Sandy answered huffily. "You just practically made a fool of me every time I pitched a ball. What's that to get mad at?"

"I wasn't trying to make a fool of you."

"What were you trying to do?"

"Strengthen your game. How're you going to do a good job against some real competition if you have it all your own way in practice?"

"So you were doing me a favor. You just about ruined my game and now you pass it all off as a favor." Sandy was working herself up into a fine sense of righteous indignation. "I suppose you'll be out there when we play Brighthaven, sitting on the bleachers and shouting your head off to our deadly rivals, telling them just how to score against me."

"I wouldn't do any such thing!" Now he was indignant. "You think I haven't got any sense of honor? Why, I'll be there cheering for you."

"I hope you won't be there at all."

"Look here," he said. "You're taking this thing too personally."

"Personally? Taking it too personally?"

"Yes, ma'am. You're too touchy. You get offended too quickly. I could see that this afternoon."

Sandy backed him toward the door as she answered. "And the trouble with you is that you're a buttinsky. I've known you two whole weeks. Two whole weeks, and what have you done in that short time? You've butted in on every sandlot game. You barged in here last night and invited yourself to supper."

"I did not invite myself to supper. Your sister asked me."

She ignored the correction. "Then today you had to come out to softball practice. Uninvited." She almost hissed the word. "That in itself wasn't enough. You had to take over the game, force yourself upon the poor B team, do all their thinking for them. I may be touchy, but you certainly are the most conceited, the most"—she floundered for a word strong enough and recalled a phrase she had read in an essay for literature—"the most egregiously egotistical boy I've ever met."

There was a moment's silence in the kitchen as the phrase sank in. She was only vaguely aware of what it meant.

He did nothing at first, and when he did act, it was slowly, in that deliberate way he had. He smiled his crooked smile, brushed back the lock of wavy hair that dipped over his forehead, and held out his hand.

"Now," he said amiably, "let's be friends. I've called you a name and you've called me a bigger one, so let bygones be bygones."

She accepted his hand in a short, brief clasp. "Okay," she said. "The scrap is over."

She expected now that he would go home and perhaps she would never be bothered by him again. Not so!

"Look," he said, "I understand you've got quite a fondness for horses."

"Who told you that?" Then she knew before he could answer. "Oh, Ran. He blabs everything."

"How'd you like to come over to Bartons' with me? I'm heading there now. They've got some good horses."

"I know," she nodded. The Bartons were the only people in town who owned horses. They lived in a big house on over a hundred acres of land. Sometimes she had seen the Barton girls home from college riding along the country roads, and she had always felt a twinge of envy. She would have given anything to be riding one of those horses.

"I've got a job with the Bartons," Bill went on. "All summer. The girls are going to Europe and there won't be anyone at the house who rides. They want someone to help the caretaker look after the horses and exercise them."

"You mean you're going over to the Bartons' every day?"

"That's it. Want to come along tonight? I've got my uncle's car."

It was quite a temptation. A few years back she used to say to herself, "If I only owned a horse." At that time, owning a horse, being able to ride every day, had seemed the most desirable thing in life. Greg had taken her over to Eastport several times, where two men had started a riding academy. For so much an hour you could hire a horse and one of the men would watch you ride and correct the things you did wrong. The man in charge had taken to Sandy from the start. He'd say, "Here's the girl who knows how to handle a horse." And he would pay special attention to her riding. Those had been star-studded trips over to Eastport, and Sandy almost wept the day Greg said they couldn't go any more because the academy was closing up. There weren't enough customers and they couldn't make a go of it. Sandy had taken a bus over to Eastport to say good-by to the man who ran the stables and to have one last ride on her favorite horse, but she was too late. They had all cleared out. Only the empty stables remained, and she had walked through them desolate, swinging open the gates of the stalls and feeling like running away from home after the horses and that chunky little man who had taught her to ride.

She did not run after them. She went home and tried to forget. She did not forget, either. For months she grieved over her loss and collected horse pictures and teased Greg to take her to Brampton where there was another academy, but Brampton was too far, Greg pointed out. It was a whole day's trip coming and going.

So tonight Wyoming Bill was holding out a shining temptation to her. Something in her eyes must have told him what an attractive invitation it was, because he repeated it.

"I'd be glad to have you come along."

This quick forgiveness, this willingness to let bygones be bygones and start out afresh after the tongue-lashing she had given him, was something quite new to her. She did not understand it, but she was willing to accept him as he was. And she wanted very much to go to the Barton stables. She ran to the door and bellowed up the back stairs to Marlene, "Bill wants me to go to the Barton house with him. He's got a job looking after the horses. Can I?"

"How late will you be?" Sandy turned to Bill for the answer to Marlene's question.

"Not so very," he called up the stairs. "Ought to be back before ten o'clock."

"All right. Have a good time." There was a pleased note in Marlene's voice. Then, as a motherly afterthought she added from years of habit, "Don't forget your jacket."

2

ON THE ride out to the estate, Bill was his usual friendly and loquacious self. He wanted to know about Sandy's name. It interested him. Where had she picked up that nickname? He wondered if it had originated in the sandlot on Gardner Street, which he understood had been her favorite stamping grounds since she was knee-high to a prairie dog.

"No, it isn't because of the sandlot," she said. Then she told him about the Herzog names. Their mother had named them after movie stars. Marlene, Gregory, Randolph, Sandra.

"Sandra. Why, that's a real pretty name. I like it."

"Maybe you do," she said flatly. "But I don't. You better never call me that if you want to be friends."

"All right, you win, Sandy." He looked ahead at the road. "You sure make up your mind fast and never change it, don't you?"

"You've got to have backbone," she told him. "If you don't stand up for what you think is right, everybody pushes you around. That's what my dad always says."

"I haven't met your father. Ran says he travels a lot. He's a sales engineer, isn't he?"

"That's right. He's away six, eight weeks at a stretch."

"Good thing you've got Marlene and Greg to look after you."

"Sure, I guess so. Greg's swell. I'm nuts about him. You think it's wrong to make a hero of your own brother?"

"Not a brother like Greg."

"He can do anything. Everything. Skis, swims like a champion, plays a good game of baseball, was football captain at high. Greg's one in a million. Only he's an awful tease."

"Most brothers are."

"Marlene's all right in her way," Sandy said. "She likes to run things, though. Especially me. Complains about my grooming. My *grooming.* Imagine! I haven't got any. I just wash my face and comb my hair and put on some clothes."

"Marlene's beautiful."

"Sure she's beautiful, and she thinks everyone else should try to be. Me, I'll never be a beauty." She mimicked Marlene's voice, " 'If only you'd wear some decent clothes, Sandy. Take off those filthy jeans and sneakers and do something about your face!' " Sandy snorted. "I always say to her, 'What am I going to do about it? It's the only face I've got.' "

"And what does Marlene say?"

"She says," and again she mimicked, " 'Any face can be made interesting, even if it isn't pretty.' Marlene heard that in a movie once. So I say to her, 'Interesting! What do you want me to do? Hang a couple of carrots from my ears and paint green dots on my nose?' She says

I'm fresh. I guess maybe I am sometimes. But she makes me mad. Buys silly dresses for me. All ruffles and bows and fancy gadgets on them. She still thinks I'm a baby or a doll that she can dress up. I won't wear the stuff. Got a whole closet full, but I hate those fancy dresses."

She was wound up, talking fast, more than she usually did about her family. It was something in Bill, a relaxed and sympathetic quality that seemed to release these pent-up emotions.

"I'm talking too much," she said.

"No, go ahead. I like it."

She leaned forward. "Isn't that the estate just ahead?" Bill nodded. "Whew!" she exclaimed. "Some cozy little shack."

The Barton house was one of those anachronisms that had been built into a small New England town by a soda-pop baron in the late 1800s. It had once been the very heart of the town, but the town had grown and the Barton estate had remained static, so that now it was pushed off to one side, alone and quite formidable in its medieval splendor.

You approached it, as Bill did tonight, by swinging your car up a long, long drive bordered with towering maples and elms. A blight had ravaged some of the elms and they, like the huge baronial house, proclaimed that they had seen better days.

The "mansion"—because that is what so many people in New Sharon still called the Barton house—had never pretended to be any special style of architecture. It was just big. Big and impressive. Those were the ideas the owner had in mind when he built it, importing marble and tile and paneling from halfway around the world to complete his nightmare of shockingly bad taste.

To Sandy, the Barton estate had always been a glamorous world. "Been inside?" she asked Bill.

"No," he answered. "Only the caretaker's house."

He drove some distance beyond the house and pulled up in front of a stone building. "The stables," he explained, getting out.

She was already half out of the car, and Bill, who had run around to open the door, smiled at her eagerness.

"We'd better take some good will along," he said, reaching into the car and pulling out a bunch of carrots. He handed her a couple and she stuffed them into her pockets.

They stopped a moment at the caretaker's house and Sandy was introduced to Fred, a stocky man with nice eyes, dark wavy hair that was receding across his broad forehead, and an altogether pleasant manner. Sandy noticed that he limped slightly and guessed that was why Bill had to curry the horses.

"So you've brought along your girl," Fred said.

Sandy would have denied being anybody's girl but Bill saved her the trouble. "Just a horse-crazy friend," he said, winking at Sandy.

"Good," said Fred. "I like people who like horses."

It was quickly revealed that Fred was from the Midwest —Iowa—that he had lived on a farm as a boy, that he had come East to study art years ago, that it hadn't worked out, that he had shifted around a good deal, and that now he had settled down here as the Barton's caretaker. He liked it. He liked being around horses. He liked being let alone a good deal of the time. He could draw a little, fuss around with his charcoal sketches, paint a few pictures when he had a mind to, and life was not bad at that.

"But now we've talked enough about me," he said in a resonant voice Sandy liked. "Let's look at the horses."

"They used to have twelve, fifteen horses in here," Fred explained as they entered the stables. "Quite a come-down to be keeping only four."

I'd be satisfied with just one! Sandy thought.

"They've been fed," Fred said. "But Lucky Lady's waiting for her treat." He turned to Sandy, laughing. "Lucky Lady's got a crush on him," and he nodded toward Bill. "She's that handsome bay horse in the end stall. A thoroughbred."

Sandy was on edge with excitement. It was always this way when she got around horses. It had been this way out in Eastport at the riding academy. "Horsy," Greg teasingly called her. If being "horsy" was loving these handsome animals with the big dark eyes and beautiful expressions, she guessed Greg was right.

Just now she did not know where to look first. To be confronted by four handsome horses, each one finer than the other, was almost too much to bear. She let her eyes race from one stall to the other while her mind raced along with them. She wanted to ride them all—the roan mare in the first stall and the sturdy brown fellow in the second stall, the one with the tremendous shoulders and long back, and the gentle filly with the proud head and long mane next to him, and. . . .

Sandy interrupted her thoughts as her eyes rested on Lucky Lady in the last stall.

"I've never seen such a horse," she said, almost reverently. She was thinking of the horses at the Eastport academy and she could see now what poor specimens they had been. Whatever these were—and she knew only that Lucky Lady was a thoroughbred because Fred had told her so—they were purebred animals.

"These are horses!" she exclaimed again, locking her hands behind her and strutting the length of the stables because she was too full of excitement to keep still.

She watched Bill. Until now he had stayed out of the picture, letting Fred do all the talking. Now suddenly she realized that for all Bill's quietness, the horses had been keenly aware of him. That pricking up of Lucky Lady's ears was for Bill only. The roan was whinnying, talking to him, calling that she had been waiting for him.

He started down the line of stalls, handing out carrot tidbits as he went. Lucky Lady was impatient. She stamped in her stall, tossing her head, making soft protesting noises.

"She's the prima donna," Fred said. "She wants all the attention."

A loud telephone bell, outside the caretaker's house, set up an insistent clang. Fred hurried toward the door. "Stop by at the house," he called back. "I'll give you a bottle of soda before you leave." Popping his head back in, he added, "I've had Glamour Girl and Leisure out in the paddock for a few hours. You take care of the Lady and Gadabout."

With Bill busy at Lucky Lady's stall, Sandy went over to read the names on each stall. Glamour Girl was the filly, Leisure the roan mare, Gadabout the sturdy horse with the tremendous front and shoulders. Sandy broke off some pieces of carrot and went up to the roan mare and offered her a bit. The roan accepted it, but by the way she tossed her head in Bill's direction, Sandy knew it would have tasted better if Bill had offered it.

Bill led Lucky Lady from the stall and started tacking her up. Sandy was immediately at his side, watching every movement he made. He handled the horse even better than the chunky little groom out at the Eastport academy, and although it was clear that this mare was a high-strung lady, she let Bill put on the bridle and saddle.

"Can I ride with you?" Sandy asked.

Bill looked her over. She could almost read his thoughts. He was thinking she didn't know the first thing about horses. But he said, "Even if I said yes, you're not dressed for it." He glanced at her trousers.

"I wore these when I rode over in Eastport."

"Those slacks will ride up on you and be darned uncomfortable," Bill stubbornly objected. She didn't argue back. She had a feeling that if she kept quiet, he would soften and let her ride. He fussed with the martingale on Lucky Lady. He was very thorough, going over the horse and the equipment to be sure they were ready.

Then after a minute or two he turned to Sandy and said, "All right. You can take Gadabout out."

"I want to ride the Lady," she said.

"You want to ride the Lady." There was no surprise

in Bill's voice, only a kind of amused superiority. It nettled Sandy. His next words irritated her even more than his voice. "The Lady's too much horse for a beginner."

"You think I don't know how to handle a horse. You're wrong. The man at Eastport said I was very quick to learn. He said I had good hands and good legs and—and"—in her eagerness to justify herself, she stammered—"and a feeling for a horse."

"That's fine," Bill said, with that same superior tone in his voice, "but has the horse got a feeling for you?" She turned away from him, angry to be frustrated about riding the Lady. "Look," he went on. "This is quite a lot of horse. She's mettlesome, to begin with. She'd be hard to handle even if she'd been trained right. But she hasn't been trained right. The Bartons took her off some friend's hands because no one in the friend's family could handle her."

Sandy turned back, all ears. "You mean she's got vices?"

"I mean she's head-shy. Look." He ran his hand over the Lady's forehead and she drew back, shaking her head. "Even I can't get familiar, and she likes me." He went over to the stall and picked up the Lady's blanket. "Look at this." It was torn in several places. "And," he concluded, "how would you handle a horse that reared under the saddle?" He paused. "I don't mean a horse that rears intentionally because she's mean. I mean a horse that's so scared at times that she will come over backward with the rider if you don't handle her right."

Sandy was impressed. "All right," she said, "I'll ride Gadabout."

"Tack him up." Bill gave the order in a businesslike tone.

You're not back home in Wyoming giving orders to the hands on your father's ranch, Sandy thought, but she went over to Gadabout's stall. Although she had helped tack up her horse at Eastport, she had never managed it alone. She felt that Bill was testing her, trying to find out just how much she knew about handling horses, and she knew she had to pass this first test or he'd never have any confidence in her again.

She took down the bridle and slipped it over Gadabout's head. Her hands shook a little but Gadabout was a patient horse, the very opposite of the Lady, and he did not seem to notice the way Sandy's hands fumbled. She did a little better with the saddle. There were several English saddles hanging there but she chose a Western saddle, the kind Bill used, and she was thorough like Bill, making sure the saddle was in place, testing the girth for the right degree of tightness by running her fingers under it. Bill watched her, but said nothing.

"All set?" he asked when he thought she had dallied long enough. "Let's go."

They rode out into the soft air of early evening, following the bridle path through the Barton estate. Bill rode beside her, adjusting his pace to hers. This was a new world for Sandy. The path led them into a woodsy stretch of land which, in this springtime of the year, was alive with activity. Around and above them were the invisible dwellers in this place of ancient evergreens and wild-growing maples and oaks. Sandy listened to the evening calls of birds, sweet and poignant to the ear, with the sad song of the wood thrush dominating. She heard the scurry of startled animals, squirrels and chipmunks and woodchucks. A brown thrasher darted out and flew in front of them.

Sandy and Gadabout got along fine. He was dependable and free of temperament, not even trying Sandy out to see if he could get away with anything, the way so many horses will at first. And she could see, as they rode along, why Bill had refused to let her ride the Lady. She would go along quietly for a while and then begin to cut capers. Sandy knew enough about horses to sense the dormant excitement boiling up inside the Lady. Anything, even the littlest stir along the ground, would frighten her. It was obvious that only Bill's excellent horsemanship kept her under control, and her prancings and high spirits were all the more noticeable beside the steady jogging of Gadabout.

Bill was a different boy along the trail. She had come to think of him as a good-natured meddler, adept at the art of gate-crashing, a boy with plenty of selling ability, plenty of charm. This first evening of riding revealed a new Bill. In the saddle he grew serious, almost silent and moody. Occasionally he spoke to the horses, or to her, reminding her not to let Gadabout stop to nibble grass.

But on the whole, his thoughts seemed to be elsewhere. He rode so effortlessly that, even with the temperamental Lady, he could afford to relax. Sandy watched Bill, wondering what was on his mind. He seemed miles away from the Barton estate and from her.

They turned their horses toward home and let them walk back to the stables. Dusk was falling fast as they dismounted and led the horses in.

"End of the trail," Bill said.

The words seemed wistful, as if "end of the trail" meant something quite different from the Barton estate.

Then suddenly his mood changed as he was teaching Sandy how to put the horses up for the night. "Want to stop at Fred's for a little while?" he asked. "We still have over an hour before I promised to get you back home. Fred gets lonesome, and he can be a lot of fun."

"Sure," she said. "I'm ready for the drink he promised."

Fred gave them an openhanded welcome. He was waiting in his small living room in the caretaker's house. Sandy was surprised at how comfortable and homelike the place was.

"Why, you'd never think a man lived here alone!" she exclaimed. "It's so neat."

"It seems Sandy has a small opinion of men," Bill said.

"I didn't mean it that way," she said quickly.

Fred had the refreshments arranged on a big tray on the coffee table. There were tall glasses filled with ice, and an assortment of soda flavors to choose from, and half a fudge layer cake cut in generous slices.

"Make yourself at home," Fred said. He acted as if he liked to have them here. There was a fire in the fireplace, "because it gets damp in these stone houses on a spring evening," Fred explained. So they sat around the fire in club chairs and talked. Fred's Belgian police dog, Blackie, and his cat, Mona Lisa, joined them.

Fred drew Sandy out. He asked her to tell him about the softball at school.

Then they talked about the Barton horses, and without letting on how little she really knew, Sandy learned a lot by listening to Fred and Bill. Gadabout was a Morgan horse, a fine dependable horse for an inexperienced rider. The filly was a Kentucky saddler. She would be beautiful when full grown, not so temperamental as Lucky Lady but plenty of horse to handle at that.

They discussed Lucky Lady, filling in the parts of her background that Sandy had not known. She had been trained as a race horse early in her career, overfed and overridden, so that she became nervous and irritable. Next she had fallen into bad hands, and a sloppy groom had let her get spoiled. Then, to teach her some manners, she had been turned over to a hard-bitten old stable boy who mistreated her. That was why she was head-shy. Finally she had been bought by her previous owners, who had fallen in love with her looks at an auction, but she was too much horse for them to ride. They had given her to the Bartons.

"And that," said Fred, turning to Sandy, "is where Bill comes into the picture. He's done marvels with Lucky Lady already. He's quite a man with horses."

Sandy grunted her acquiescence. She was thinking about Lucky Lady. Out there on the bridle path tonight, she had wanted more than anything to ride her, even when she saw the horse acting up with Bill. There was something about Lucky Lady that appealed to her. It had been that way from the beginning. It was still that way as she listened to her history. She felt a kinship with this horse who had been through so much. She had seen that latent excitement boiling up in Lucky Lady and she felt that somehow it was like a seething something inside herself, a yearning to be understood, a wanting to realize herself as an individual. She's a little like me, she thought. No one understands me either. Not Marlene, with her absorption in clothes and looks and boys. Not Ran, with his nose and ears and eyes glued to his radio hobby all the time. Not Dad, who's away almost all the time on his salesman's job. Not even Greg, who can be devoted one moment and a merciless tease the next.

No one understands me, she thought. Not the real me. No one understands Lucky Lady either. Not even Bill understands her. He handles her well because he loves horses and she knows that. But he doesn't really get under the hide of her. I could, she thought. I could understand her. Maybe someday they'll let me ride her.

She voiced the thought to Bill and Fred. "I'd like to ride Lucky Lady someday."

"I never saw anyone so eager to break her own neck," Bill commented.

Fred did not laugh with Bill. He was quiet a moment and then said, "I don't know about that. I think maybe someday she'll be able to handle the Lady."

"Sure," Bill agreed. "Any day a million years from now."

They switched the conversation to other things—the feeding of the horses, the care of the stable, the odd quirks of each of the animals. The roan mare loved Fred's cat, and would not feed unless Mona Lisa was nearby. The filly would not sleep without her own plaid blanket. Once, by mistake, Fred had mixed the blankets, and Glamour Girl kept them awake for two nights until he discovered what the trouble was.

Sandy sat there, drinking it all in. Horse talk. She loved it. She like this place too, and she liked the middle-aged man over there with the kind eyes and genial manner. You liked him because you felt he liked you first. He's nice, she thought. He loves people. And she thought too that she would like to come back again and talk to him.

So she was glad when, as they were going, he called them into the next room to see his drawings and paintings.

"My studio," he explained. "Not big, but adequate."

Here Sandy was completely lost, because if she knew little about horses and their handling, she knew nothing about art. Yet, for Fred's sake, she admired his "stuff," as he called it. There were quite a few charcoal sketches of heads. "I go to a sketching class," Fred explained. "We hire a model every week." There were some Midwestern landscapes and Sandy liked these best of all.

"It's my one indulgence," Fred said. "I paint them from my boyhood memories."

Bill stood before one large canvas, a scene of rolling fields with one tiny house, a startling red dot, lost in the middle of tall brown-tasseled corn.

"No one can forget what he came from," Bill said.

"You try to forget and you can't. There's something that pulls you back. Back to those open places out there."

As Bill talked Sandy felt pushed away from them, as if they were no longer here with her. It was the same feeling she had had at the end of the ride when they came through the dusk to the stables and Bill had said, with all that wistfulness inside him, "End of the trail."

Then, in a twinkling, the nostalgic spell was broken. "Look, Sandy," Fred said, "how about letting me do a portrait of you?"

"Of me!" She laughed. "My sister Marlene's the one you should sketch. She's beautiful." Then, as if she needed substantiation, she added, "Everyone says so."

"But I want to paint you," Fred said. "You've got a face you don't see on everybody."

"I'm sure," Sandy said, "that everybody is glad of that."

Fred turned to Bill. "Don't you think she's a fine-looking girl, Bill?"

"Sure," Bill said. "If she weren't, I wouldn't have brought her over here tonight."

Sandy was a trifle dismayed by all this attention. She would much rather have Marlene standing here berating her for her sloppiness and lack of grooming than hear all this palaver about being fine-looking. She knew what she looked like without anyone telling her. She was plump and funny-looking. All the girls at school said she was just comical to look at.

"When will you bring her back again, Bill, so I can make a sketch of our girl friend?"

"Tomorrow," Bill said.

"I'll come back to ride Gadabout but I won't have my picture painted. Not me!" She was very positive, and she edged toward the door as she spoke.

Fred laughed away her ungraciousness and she felt ashamed that she had made so flat a refusal.

"If you let me ride Lucky Lady," she said, "I'll let you do my picture."

"A horse trader," Fred said. "Just a Yankee horse trader, Bill. That's what Sandy is." The party broke up. Fred's voice followed them as they ran out to Bill's car.

"See you tomorrow," he called. "Take care."

They turned down the driveway and drove out of the estate. It was pitch-black along the path and only the headlights of the car lighted the road for them.

"I like Fred," Sandy said. "He's a real guy."

She was surprised when she threw open the back door of her house to find the whole family waiting for her.

"I'm on time," she said defensively. "It's not ten yet."

"Did you have fun?" Marlene asked. There was eagerness in her voice. "Why didn't you bring Bill in?"

Sandy went to the refrigerator and opened the door. She kept her back to them while she took out what she wanted—a bottle of milk and a piece of pie. She felt the eyes of the whole family turned upon her even though she could not see them. She wanted to burst out laughing. So that was it. They thought she had a boy friend. She could hear them talking it over. "At last Sandy's got a boy friend. At last." What a relief for them. The poor ugly duckling of a kid who wouldn't dress up and who was chunky and had a face that made people want to chuckle in amusement. The kid had a boy friend at last.

"Did you have fun, Sandy?" Marlene repeated.

"Sure. I rode a Morgan horse. Gadabout's his name. And we went over to see Fred."

"Fred?"

"Sure. The caretaker at Barton's. He's all right."

"Oh." Although Marlene did not add it, Sandy could imagine her thinking, "Rode a horse and visited the caretaker. That couldn't have been much fun."

All right, Sandy thought. Here goes.

With her mouth full of pie she turned around and faced them. "I'm going back tomorrow," she gulped. "Bill asked me to. And Fred wants to paint a picture of me. He's an artist. He says I have an interesting face. The kind you don't see on everybody."

Greg was grinning and even Ran was watching with interest, but it was Marlene's face that Sandy stared into as she went on, because Marlene's mouth was wide open and her eyes filled with the utmost incredulity.

Sandy grimaced, in imitation of Fred. "He turned my head this way and then he turned it that. 'Interesting,' he said. So I told him he was barking up the wrong tree, that it's my sister Marlene he ought to paint. She's beautiful, I told him." Sandy made a flourish, warming to her subject as she spoke. "So he turned to Bill and asked him if he didn't think I was a fine-looking girl."

"And what," Marlene asked, "did Bill say?"

"He said sure he did. If he hadn't thought so, he wouldn't have asked me over to see the horses."

3

THERE were times in the next few days when Sandy would try to stop and think what life had been like before she knew Bill. It couldn't have been less than a week ago. Why, it seemed as if they had known each other forever.

Besides being one of the most intense and headlong friendships on record, it was perhaps one of the most extraordinary. Sandy was well aware too that it was a friendship that was being watched by many curious eyes. At school the girls tried to classify it, and Sandy secretly gloated over the fact that they could not.

Friendships, it appeared, had to fall into categories. When a boy and a girl liked each other there were traditional patterns of behavior to be followed.

The girls wanted to know why Bill did not write notes to Sandy and pass them to her in the halls. They wondered why he did not hound her footsteps, waiting for her after classes, walking through the corridors with her, stopping outside the classroom for a few precious moments before the bell rang. He should be looking at her with his heart in his eyes. He should give her something. The large gold ring with the deep garnet stone he wore on his right hand, or even something less binding, like one of his Western neckerchiefs. Sandy was not a glamour girl with whom a boy might fall easily in love, they admitted, but everyone was attractive to someone, and there were very few girls in the school who possessed so much cheerfulness and pep. So if Bill had taken to her he ought to show it in some concrete ways.

Bill, oblivious to the comment he was causing in the feminine quarters of New Sharon High, went blithely on his way having the kind of friendship with Sandy that he wanted. Sandy, being Sandy, liked it better that way. If Bill had been a boy who deluged her with the usual masculine attentions, mooning over her in the halls and staring her out of countenance at assemblies and writing her silly notes (she had seen some of these displayed by simpering girls, beginning "Hon" or "Doll" or even "Darling" and running through such inept remarks as "Wasn't last night super?" and "I think of you every hour on the hour" and notes empurpled with phrases and titles from popular songs and signed "Fondly" or "With love") —if he had written such nonsense and talked such nonsense and offered her his ring or his neckerchief, she would have been so embarrassed that she would never have wanted to speak to him again.

As it was, Bill and she did not see very much of each other while school was in session. Being in different years, they had no classes together. If they happened to pass each other, he would wave casually and call a friendly "Hi!" That was all. In the cafeteria, he ate at a table with all boys. The boys liked him and he had already established several loyal friendships. In school Bill was a man among men, and Sandy rejoiced that this was so.

Then, after school was out, Bill became New Sharon's most famous spectator sports fan. It was a standing joke within a short time that wherever the high school played a game, Bill would turn up. Too late to participate in active sports, he became a vigorous supporter at baseball, track, tennis, softball. The baseball team made him their mascot, taking the leggy Westerner along when they played away from New Sharon. Sometimes they let him keep score. But always his voice with its inimitable drawl could be heard booming above all the others in the bleachers.

He did not show up the rest of that week at softball practice. Sandy was not sorry. She doubted that he could have curbed his enthusiasm for meddling into other people's business. He would have taken over much as he had before, and that would have put quite a strain on their friendship. Maybe, Sandy reasoned, that was why he stayed away.

He did not, however, stay away from the Herzog house. Every evening, like clockwork, the same little scene would be enacted. While Sandy was still drying and stacking the dishes, Bill would come around the side of the house, whistling. You could catch sight of his lean form through the windows, his hands in his pockets, his Stetson cocked back on his head. Then he would stop outside the back screen door. He never knocked, but with his hat crumpled in his hand, he would call, "Is anybody home?"

Everybody was "home" to Bill. Greg would saunter in from the dining room where he had been accomplishing the difficult feat of watching television and reading a newspaper at the same time. Marlene, lovely and radiant even in a kitchen apron, would throw open the door and say, "Why, Bill it's you. Come on in. I've saved you a piece of pie. Strawberry and rhubarb tonight." Then Ran would come clattering down the stairs, yelling long before he came in sight, "Bill, is that you? Come on upstairs. I'm getting Bermuda."

Bill would eat his pie, rapidly and efficiently, scraping the plate with his fork because it was "so darn good," but he would not go upstairs with Ran.

"I've come to collect Sandy," he would say, making her feel like a horse being collected before a gallop through the park. "We've got a date." He always called it a date and always made it seem spontaneous, although they were going to do the same thing as they had the night before and the night before that.

No matter how many times they went over to the Barton stables, Sandy was sure she would never get tired of it. After a few days, the horses knew her. Bill was still the great favorite, but they liked her too.

Gadabout made a real fuss over her. You would think he was her horse. She always brought him some treat, something green from the vegetable box in the Herzog refrigerator, and they would talk to each other while she gave him this special delicacy.

They would ride out every evening. Sometimes they took the bridle path through the estate, but as Bill gained more confidence in Sandy they ventured farther still, along the country roads of the town, passing meadows and fields and woodsy spots, stopping at a bend in the road where the river came up to meet the road to let Gadabout and Lucky Lady or Leisure or Glamour Girl have a drink. Bill rode a different horse each night, but Gadabout was always reserved for Sandy.

On these early evening rides she learned a lot from Bill. He taught her the importance of balance, not only in the rider, but in the horse too. He showed her how to relax her ankles by having the stirrup iron on the ball of her foot and placing her foot as close as she could to the inner side of the iron. "Sit straight," he would say. "Keep your back easy and your shoulders square and your chin up, with your eyes looking ahead between your horse's ears. And remember, good legs are as important as good hands. Lots of riders place too much emphasis on good hands."

He taught her how to use the aids without making a great fanfare and flourish over every movement. "The horse will respond more readily to relaxed signals, Sandy."

They practiced the walk, the trot, the canter.

"When will you teach me to jump?" she asked him one evening.

"You Eastern riders are plumb crazy about jumping. Out"—he paused a minute, then rushed on—*"out home,* a horse isn't forced to jump when it isn't necessary." Then he said something that surprised her. "Horses are not natural jumpers, Sandy. They've learned how to do it well, but it's not natural for them." Sandy did not press the point. She had learned to bide her time with Bill.

Every evening when they came back to the stables she would linger at Lucky Lady's stall. Bill would eye her as she stood there, watching the beautiful bay horse with the white streak above her nose.

"Are you stalking your prey?" he once asked her, and Sandy flushed that he had so accurately read what was on her mind. She was waiting, waiting. Someday I'll ride her, she thought with a fierceness that pushed against her from inside. Someday they'll have to let me ride her.

Sandy and Bill always stopped by to see Fred, if only for a few moments, and he never let up his coaxing to do a portrait of her.

"When you let me ride Lucky Lady," she would say. It became favorite repartee between them. It was their greeting, the first thing Fred would say to her, the first thing she would answer. Then, as they would get ready to leave he would call out, "Don't forget to come back so I can make a sketch of you."

Her voice, sailing clear through the soft spring air, would answer, "When you let me ride the Lady!"

4

THE softball diamond turned its dusty, sand-beige face to the midafternoon sun as Sandy raced across it. Having talked good-natured Miss Ives, her English teacher, into letting her out ten minutes early to change her clothes, Sandy was almost the first one on the field.

Getting ready for a softball game involved certain details that had become almost a ritual to Sandy. First she had to put on a clean white shirt for every game, no matter if it would be smeared with dirt and soaked with perspiration in five minutes. She had to begin clean. She had to wear a certain pair of blue denim trousers, too. They were not her own. Once last year she had borrowed them from Ellie Winchester who was a size or two smaller, so the trousers were snug-fitting on Sandy and faded to grayish-white, yet nothing would persuade her to abandon them. These were the denim pants she had worn the day Miss MacDonald had said for the first time, "All right, Sandy. Go in and pitch. Let's see what you can do."

And she had won the game for her school.

This afternoon she ran across the field in an outburst

of jubilant spirits, shouting greetings to Ellie, whose job as team manager had brought her out early too.

"We're sure going to win today!" she called out. "Brighthaven will be a pushover."

Brighthaven was never a pushover in anything, least of all softball. But it made her feel confident to shout that to Ellie, and this afternoon she had that feeling of victory that sometimes comes to players before a game. It was all part of her feeling that the world—today, at least—was very right. Things were going her way, no mistake about it. She had just received 92 in a history test and 96 in an English test. Tonight, after the game, she had a date to go out to the Barton estate. Gadabout was waiting for her there, and so was Lucky Lady. On the bed of her room at home lay a new pair of frontier-style riding pants, a gift from Greg, whose payday had been yesterday. "Strictly an advance birthday present," he had warned her. "So don't try to collect in July." She would wear the new pants tonight. There were other things to be grateful for. These evenings with Bill had mushroomed into something tremendously important to her. She enjoyed not only the ride, but the visits afterward when they stopped at Fred's place for refreshments. Fred treated her differently from the way anyone else had ever treated her. Everyone else was always laughing at her or scolding her. Fred did neither. He did not find her the buffoon so many schoolmates did. He did not upbraid her about her appearance the way Marlene did. He didn't tease her as Greg did or try to ignore her the way Ran did.

Once, on the way home, trying to explain her liking for Fred to Bill, she had said, "He treats me grown-up. You don't notice how much older he is. When I'm around Fred, I feel as if I ought to get some manners for a change."

He would help her off with her jacket when she came in, and hold it for her when she put it on to leave. He would pull out a chair for her. Once or twice she had run into the studio to look at something and he would stand up when she returned and keep standing until she sat down. He always served her before Bill, saying, "Ladies first."

"Lady," she said laughingly to Bill. "He calls me a *lady!*"

So today, riding on the crest as she surely was, she was certain they would give Brighthaven the shellacking of that school's long and illustrious career.

The field was gradually filling up. Sandy helped Ellie place the bats in a row near the home plate. She helped check over the balls and mitts piled up near the rocky slab of ledge that made an ideal place for the girls to throw down their jackets and relax while the other team was up at bat. Then she stood around, waiting for Dodo to show up so they could warm up before the game. She stood as solidly as one of the rocks at her back, her hands on her hips, her feet spread apart, her eyes surveying with a proprietary sense the field around her.

This is it! her mind was singing. This is a swell reason for being alive!

She watched the yellow bus, chartered by the visiting

team, disgorge its crew of girls from Brighthaven. Wendy Mason, the New Sharon captain, ran over to chat with a couple of girls she knew from the rival school.

Then Dodo Frazer, clad in brown shorts and a drab brown shirt, came reluctantly across the field.

"She looks as if she were going to a funeral," Sandy said to Carol Soltesz, the varsity first baseman. Carol laughed and Sandy called out a cheerful "Hi, Grumpy!" to Dodo. "Come on, let's warm up."

Dodo, unsmiling, went to the catcher's box. She examined the catcher's mitt with mournful suspicion, as if she expected a snake to pop out at her.

Sandy, on the pitcher's plate, tried out her arm. It was fit as a fiddle. She went through her usual routine, warming up her comedy antics as well as her pitching arm. Her grimaces made no impression on the sober-faced Dodo, who got ready to catch with about as much enthusiasm as if a bomb were about to be hurled at her.

After two or three pitches, with the ball poised in her right hand, Sandy stopped.

"Hey," she called to Carol Soltesz. "Look who's going to umpire."

Miss MacDonald and Mrs. Sherman, the Brighthaven coach, were talking to a slender girl with tight curly hair and bright blue eyes. The girl was nervous, straining to please, and although she wore the regulation jacket of a well-known physical education college, she was plainly new at the business of umpiring.

"Jeanne Hadley," Carol said to Sandy. "She's home for the week end."

Sandy was not thrilled by the sight of Jeanne Hadley. Last year Jeanne had been active in sports at New Sharon. She was good enough with a hockey stick or at sinking a ball into the basket or at swinging a bat, but her manner was neither forceful nor positive enough for an umpire.

Brighthaven lined up to take its place at bat. Miss MacDonald was calling out the starting line-up. Sandy could hear her voice above the kidding that was going on around them. "If everyone will just keep her eye on the ball," she said. "Never mind the runner. Watch the bases more."

A small girl with a huge letter B on her sweatshirt stepped up to bat. Sandy, wildly chewing gum, went into one of her most flamboyant windups. Dodo, not changing one iota her gloomy expression, signaled Sandy to make it a high target. The Brighthaven girl appeared nervous. Sandy released the ball and the batter let it go by.

"Strike." Jeanne Hadley's voice was so faint you could hardly hear it.

Sandy wound up again, this time using an incurve that took the batter by surprise. Again the umpire called, "Strike!"

Sandy took her time on the next one, making the little girl with the big B sweat it out. Finally she wound up and let it go. The batter fanned and Jeanne's voice, not quite sure of itself, called, "Out!"

Sandy rubbed her free hand on her faded blue trousers. This, she thought, is going to be the easiest victory yet. These Brighthaven gals don't even try.

The next girl at bat looked as easy as the first. She was big and clumsy, a top-heavy girl with hair that kept getting into her eyes.

She looks, thought Sandy, as if she wouldn't know enough to come in out of the rain.

Dodo signaled Sandy to pitch low and close to the belt.

Sandy followed Dodo's suggestion, expecting to hear Jeanne's voice call, "Strike." She was surprised when the girl hit the ball into the infield. Sandy recovered from her pitch, but too late to do any good. She ran and grabbed the ball just as the tall batter reached first base.

The Brighthaven girls roared their approval. "Nice going, Midge," they shouted. "Good girl! That's showing them!"

All right, Sandy thought. So they think they're smart.

The top-heavy girl with the faraway look had tricked her. She had played Sandy's own game, bluffing it out, playing one deception against another, and she had beat Sandy at it.

I won't be caught twice, Sandy thought.

She tightened up her game. Deadpan Dodo was the utmost help. Together they struck out the next two batters. It really wasn't much trouble when you put your mind to it.

The Brighthaven pitcher and catcher were warming up as New Sharon lined up at the bottom of the first inning. Ellie went down the line, reading off the batting order to the team. Always alerted for a new twist, a new technique, Sandy watched the Brighthaven pitcher. This one was a slender blonde with excellent coordination.

She had style and grace. She reminded Sandy of the posters in the physical education office of girls showing the right way to swing a bat, the right way to hold a hockey stick. She was the "perfect athlete" type.

Pat Manero was up at bat first. Pat swung the bat nonchalantly as she waited for the signal to play ball. The nonchalance was not a pose. Pat had been swinging bats with her five brothers and twelve cousins since she had been able to hold one. There were three Maneros on the boys' baseball team right now.

The Brighthaven pitcher threw a fast ball and Pat let it go by. "Strike!" the umpire called.

Sandy thought, "That sure looked like a ball to me." But since Miss MacDonald did not protest, Sandy kept her opinion to herself.

Again the New Sharon pitcher delivered, a low, fast ball aiming for a target she expected tall Pat Manero to miss, but Pat was ready for the low ball and this time she swung, batting the ball into the outfield. As it rolled to a stop, the outfielder picked it up and tried to decide where to throw it, but Pat's long legs were racing around the diamond. She made second base before the ball caught up with her, sliding in just before the second baseman could tag her.

The cheers from the New Sharon side were earsplitting. "Atta girl, Pat! Nice going, Pat!" Even with all the shouting Sandy could recognize a familiar voice from the bleachers. She looked over there. Bill, arriving late because of a study hall detention, was just climbing up to his favorite spot on the benches.

He was waving his big hat at the New Sharon team and shouting his encouragement.

Dodo was the next one up. Sandy watched the pitcher and the catcher as they sized Dodo up, and she laughed to herself as she thought how wrong they were going to be. Dodo's listless manner and sad expression gave the impression that she was worried sick and that her mind wasn't on the game. Quite often when Sandy looked at Dodo she thought of a movie, a nature picture, she had seen of a chameleon. The lizard sat on a leaf, making itself seem harmless and almost invisible with its protective coloring. Then, with eyes that moved almost to the back of its head, it waited for its prey. Bang! Out would go its long tongue to capture an unguarded victim.

Dodo got ready for a swing at the ball, making a show of trying out her arm. Sandy grinned. She had to look away. She couldn't stand it. The act was too much for her, because she knew what was going to happen and she was so on edge over it that she had to clamp her jaw shut so she wouldn't shout out something that would give it away.

The dopes! she thought. The big, goofy dopes! Don't they know what to look out for with a short, fast batter and a man on second base?

Apparently they didn't, because Sandy could see the pitcher get ready for another of her fast balls, aimed at a high target. Dodo could see them get ready too and she played along, swinging her bat as if she would try for a hit. The pitcher released the ball. Quick as that little lizard sitting on a leaf, Dodo grabbed the bat for a bunt. She met the ball high, tapping it lightly toward first base. The pitcher, slow to recover, lost time. Pat ran to third and Dodo to first before she grabbed the ball.

The New Sharon girls screamed their heads off. The small group of New Sharon rooters, mostly the chums and the boy friends of the team, joined in. Bill's voice dominated the cheers.

"That's the way to do it," Sandy heard him shout.

Carol Soltesz was up next. Sandy watched the Brighthaven pitcher. She seemed a little tense, but she held the ball in front of her with both hands, getting ready for a change of pace. It would not be a fast ball this time. Carol got ready to swing. She was a pretty good batter, not so accurate as Pat, or so shrewd as Dodo, but her batting average was high.

The Brighthaven pitcher used a tricky windup and released the ball.

Carol swung, but the ball faded away at the plate and the umpire called, "Strike" as Carol missed it.

The pitcher let go another one, this time an incurve, and the ball spun right past Carol as she swung at it.

"Don't let her bluff you! You can do it." There were cries of encouragement as Carol shook her head and stamped nervously around.

The pitcher was steadier now. She wound up and sent a fast ball, her best, whizzing toward Carol. The ball passed Carol before she had time to swing.

"Out!" Jeanne Hadley's voice barely reached the line-up of girls at bat.

I wish she'd call them so we can hear, Sandy thought.

Wendy Mason was next. She stepped up to bat the way a glamorous star might make an entrance on the stage. She was a graceful girl with a good figure and plenty of looks. She could be a good softball player, too, when she kept her mind off her looks, which was very seldom.

The Brighthaven pitcher made short work of Wendy.

"I'm next," Sandy said, pushing her way toward the plate. The girls laughed.

"Sandy," Ellie called to her. "Push your shirt in."

"I've been trying to push it in for the last five minutes," she retorted.

She picked up a bat and swung it. She was a good batter, reversing the familiar theory that "a good pitcher is usually a poor hitter."

Sandy shifted from one foot to the other but she kept her eye on the pitcher, waiting for the windup. The pitcher took her time.

All right, make me sweat for it, Sandy thought. I can take it.

The pitcher finally let go, sending a drop ball. Sandy watched it fade away.

"Strike," the umpire called.

The pitcher delivered another one, and again the umpire called a strike. Sandy heaved her shoulders and twisted around to stare at the spectators, her face full of disgust. The crowd laughed and someone from Brighthaven shouted, "One more and she's out."

Sandy swung the bat, showing how little she cared what a Brighthaven fan might say.

The pitcher wound up and released the ball. It was

her fast ball and Sandy was ready for it. She had figured this would be it. It came at her in a spinning blur and she struck at it, meeting it squarely with a mighty whack. She heard cheers and screams from New Sharon. "Atta girl, Sandy. Run."

She was running. She didn't need anyone to tell her what to do. She let her legs fly under her, feeling the dust roll up in her mouth and nose. She touched first, saw with that instinctive sixth sense that she could make second and ran for it. Both Pat Manero and Dodo were home already, with the screams of their teammates urging them on. New Sharon was wild with joy, splitting the air with their yells.

Then, as Sandy hitched up her trousers and pushed in her shirt, she became aware of the umpire standing there waving her out.

Sandy couldn't believe her eyes. She pointed to herself. "You mean me?"

Jeanne Hadley nodded.

"Why?" Sandy demanded, taking a step forward but still keeping one foot on base.

"You didn't touch first base."

"I certainly did!" Sandy turned to the Brighthaven first baseman. "You saw me touch it," she said. The girl shrugged, looking away from the argument as if she didn't want to get involved.

Sandy was furious. She had touched first base, decidedly. There was not a doubt in her mind about it. Even now she could visualize her sneaker skidding along the edge of the bag that marked the base.

Miss MacDonald motioned Sandy off the field. She turned to the umpire. A lot of things were on the tip of Sandy's tongue. She wanted to say, "If you'd keep your eyes in your head and watch what's going on, you'd have seen me touch first base. Everyone knows you're not a good umpire. You can't call them right; you don't even call them loud enough."

She wanted to blurt out, "You better go back to college and learn softball or get a pair of eyeglasses or something."

Instead, she just walked miserably off the field, churning with emotion, furious over all the things she would like to have said and couldn't.

She did manage to let off some steam to Miss MacDonald. "Two runs we lost. Two good runs. Maybe a third too, because I sure would have got home. Chiseled out of three runs just because that Jeanne Hadley needs eyeglasses."

Miss MacDonald shushed her and she calmed down, but inwardly she still churned. She couldn't help it. It was unfair. It was a rotten break. It was bad enough when the umpire called a legal out on you, but this was all wrong.

She slumped down on the bench and stewed and fretted. Miss MacDonald was looking over at her. This was not the first time Sandy had acted this way. She always got upset when an umpire did something she thought wrong. It stirred her up so much that she lost control. She got so angry that she wasn't any good out there on the pitcher's plate. The girls tried to talk some sense into her but it didn't help. The damage was done.

It was time to go in and pitch against Brighthaven at the top of the next inning. Miss MacDonald stood over Sandy, watching and waiting. "Do you think you can make it, Sandy?" she asked.

"I don't know," she said, looking down at her shaking hands. "I'm so mad at what that umpire did. I don't know if I can pitch."

Miss MacDonald nodded as if she understood. The girls tried to talk to Sandy, tried to brace her up.

"Let her alone," Miss MacDonald said. "Don't bother her." She turned to Pat Manero. "Go in and pitch this one, Pat. Do the best you can."

Pat, ever willing, ran across the field. She was an excellent batter but she couldn't pitch worth sour apples. Sandy looked down at her own shaking hands. No control, she thought miserably. One rotten break in a game and I lose it all.

She sat there watching Pat give the pitching job all she had. It wasn't enough. New Sharon lost the game by a score of 3–1.

5

WEARING her frontier pants, with a new yellow rodeo neckerchief at her throat, Sandy waited for Bill on the back porch that evening.

He was whistling as he came around the side of the house, but the moment he caught sight of her he stopped. He did not smile as he said, "Hi."

"Hi," she said. "I've got new pants."

He glanced at them. "I see."

"They're special for riding," she explained. "Frontier pants. The finest cavalry twill. It said so on the tag."

"Uh-huh."

"I got them just to ride Gadabout. Now we won't have to worry about my trousers riding up." He didn't answer. "Don't you like them?" she asked.

"Sure, the pants are fine."

"Marlene left a piece of pie inside for you. Blueberry. Your favorite."

"Thanks, but I'm not very hungry tonight," he said.

He did not talk on the ride out to the Barton estate. Once Sandy said, "The game was lousy, wasn't it?" He kept his eyes straight ahead as he answered, "It certainly was."

After that Sandy gave up. If he didn't want to talk, you couldn't make him.

When they got to the stables, they found a note from Fred saying that he was going to sketching class and would Bill please coax Glamour Girl to eat some more and also check the water in all the stalls. Sandy helped Bill. She knew what was expected of her and went about getting fresh water and straightening the blankets. Once while she was feeding Gadabout some chopped apples and he was answering with soft whinnying sounds of gratitude, she said, loud enough for Bill to hear, "*You* haven't got any mood on, have you, Gadabout? You give a person a civil answer when they talk to you."

Bill gave no indication of having heard. While Bill was tacking up Lucky Lady for their evening ride Sandy asked the question she asked every night: "When can I ride her?" Usually Bill would fling back some good-natured retort like "On the seventh Sunday in next July," or "I'll let you ride her for a wedding present; how's that for a deal?"

Tonight he didn't answer, not until she repeated the question twice and then he said, "You'll have to ask Fred. He's the boss around here. I only take orders from him."

The answer came as a slight shock. Until now she had thought that Bill's mood might have had something to do with his own affairs. Perhaps he had received some disturbing news from "out home." Now she knew his moodiness was connected with her.

She went back to Gadabout and led him out of the stable. Without waiting for Bill or even looking back to see if he was following her, she walked Gadabout down the road toward the open country. When she heard Lucky Lady's hoofbeats back of her, she collected Gadabout and signaled him to canter, heading out across the familiar country roads. Lucky Lady was not far behind. She heard first the accelerated hoofbeats and then the steady pace of the horse as Bill urged her to catch up.

Now it had become a race between them, with Bill chasing the galloping Gadabout. When Sandy thought she had carried the game far enough, she pulled suddenly off the road into a cleared space by the river and let Gadabout walk down to the water's edge. Bill and Lucky Lady were close behind. She heard the snap of branches, the heavy breathing of the high-spirited horse, and then there they were beside her. She leaned over and talked to Gadabout, paying no attention to Bill. He was having a bit of a time with the Lady, trying to calm her down.

"Why did you do that?" he asked angrily. "It's an agreement between us that we ride together. Fred told you never to ride out on any of the horses without me."

"I can take care of myself, if that's what's worrying you."

"I'm not worried about you." His face was flushed with annoyance. "It's Gadabout I'm worried about."

"So I don't mean as much to you as a horse," she said.

"If anything happened to you," he said, "it would have been your own fault. You had freedom of choice. The horse had to do what you wanted him to do."

Lucky Lady was restive, eager to move on, and Bill had all he could do to hold her.

"You've upset Lucky Lady," he said.

"Lucky Lady's not the only one I've upset," she answered. He glanced away. With his head held high like that he looked something like a thoroughbred himself. He was lean and taut, clean-cut and handsome like a thoroughbred. He had something of the horse's mettle. I like him this way, she thought, even better than when he's so good-natured.

"What are you mad about?" she asked. "Why are you so peeved at me?" He didn't answer. "I'm surprised at you," she went on. "Fred says you Westerners are all so outspoken. Always give it to anyone straight from the shoulder. No punches pulled."

"Some things are hard to talk about. Especially when you like someone, and you see that person doing something that is hurting herself. You can't always find the words to talk about it."

"If you mean what happened at the game this afternoon, I guess you've already showed me plainly enough that you didn't like it."

"Sandy," he blurted out, "why did you have to go haywire over a little thing like that? It was only an umpire's decision."

"A little thing! That wasn't little. That was big. We lost two runs for sure, maybe more. I was just standing up for my rights. Is there anything wrong with that?"

"Out there on the softball diamond this afternoon, I'd say there was."

"What did I do so wrong?"

"You made me ashamed of you, Sandy. You acted like

a spoiled baby. Instead of taking the umpire's decision in your stride, you went to pieces."

"I suppose you think I should have let her say I didn't touch first base when I know I did. I *did* touch first base. I honestly did." She was wrought up again, just remembering what had happened.

"I know you touched it," Bill said quietly. "I saw you do it."

"You saw me! Then why didn't you come down and stick up for me? What are you bawling me out for now?"

"Being right isn't all that matters, Sandy. People are going to disagree with you all through life, and lots of times they'll be wrong. But you can't go to pieces over it. If we all went through life refusing to play just because something happens that we don't like we'd spend a lot of time on the benches. That's why I felt kind of ashamed for you this afternoon, sitting there sulking when you could have won the game."

She turned Gadabout around and headed him toward the road. "I guess maybe you're ashamed to ride with me too," she said bitterly. "I guess maybe you're even ashamed to know me."

She raced home, not caring about their agreement to ride together, not caring about anything. This time Bill did not race after her.

When she reached the stables she could think of only one thing. She had to get out of here before Bill came back. She didn't want to talk to him again, ever. She put Gadabout in his stall but did not stop to untack him. Let Bill do that.

She ran out and took a short cut through the woods. This way she could reach the main road without Bill being able to follow her in his car. It was getting dark. She listened to the cries of the birds as they settled down for the night, and she remembered that other night not so long ago when Bill had first brought her over this path.

At last she came out on the road. Her hands were scratched from the brier bushes she had pushed aside in her hasty plunge through the woods. Her new pants had a tear in them. The darkening hand of twilight lay over everything. A car showed its headlights and she drew back into the shadows of the trees. It was Bill's car. He went by slowly, looking ahead.

She started toward home, hurrying to get as far as she could before dark. She was not afraid. Inside, she felt only the numbness of loss. She had lost everything in one fell swoop, in no longer than it takes to throw a fast ball into the outfield.

This afternoon she had been rich. She had possessed more than any girl could wish for. Only now, as she hurried toward home, did she realize how much she had lost. She had lost Gadabout. She could never again come out here to see him. In her excitement to leave, she had not even stopped to say good-by to him. She would never again be able to stroke his neck, to feel his affectionate nuzzle and hear his whinny as she fed him pieces of carrot or apple.

She would never see Lucky Lady again, and now she would surely never ride her.

And Fred. There would be no more evenings in the

snug little caretaker's house with the fire blazing and Blackie and Mona Lisa stretched at her feet. She would never again hear Fred's hearty laugh. Fred loved so many things. People and horses and cats and dogs and good music and fine pictures. Fred had become one of her favorite persons. Now she would never see him again. In a deluge of self-condemnation, she began to regret that she had been so stubborn about not letting him paint her picture. It was such a little thing she might have done for him.

She had lost Bill too.

The thought slowed her up. Until tonight, she had considered him a good friend, but you didn't call anyone your friend who was ashamed of the things you did.

Then a car passing her slowed up. She felt it stopping behind her and her first impulse was to run, thinking it was some boys looking for excitement.

"Is that you, Sandy?" a voice called.

She turned around and recognized Fred's car. "Sandy," he called again. She walked back slowly and Fred opened the door for her. "What are you doing out here alone?" he asked.

Then, unaccountably, she felt the tears pushing their way out. She did not want to cry, but she stood there bawling like a baby. Fred let her cry it out.

"Get in," he said at last. "I'll take you home."

"I don't want to go home," she said. Then, "I never want to see or talk to him again," she said.

"If you two have had a disagreement," Fred said, "I'd better stop and see how the horses are."

"We didn't have a disagreement," Sandy replied. "We had a fight."

As Fred turned up the long driveway he asked, "What was the fight about?"

Usually she settled her own battles, not dragging anyone else in, but Fred was different. You could talk things over with him without seeming to be a baby.

So she poured out the whole thing, telling him about the game and the umpire's mistake and the lost runs and how Bill had scolded her.

Fred made no comment. He got out in front of the stables and said, "You'd better wait for me over at the house. I'll be right along. I want to talk to you before I take you home."

When he joined her in his little living room, the first thing he asked was, "How did you two ever get scrapping over such a small thing as a softball game?"

"Bill started it. He wouldn't talk to me tonight. When I asked him what he was mad about, he said I shouldn't have got upset at the game just because of a wrong decision. He admitted that he saw me touch first base. Instead of standing up for me, he bawled me out."

"And you think his attitude is all wrong."

"I certainly do. He even said he was ashamed for me, the way I acted this afternoon. I told him maybe he was ashamed even to know me and that's when I rode off and left him."

"Being ashamed *for* a person doesn't mean you're ashamed *of* him, Sandy. It might mean the very opposite. A boy might be so fond of a girl that when she does something wrong, something that seems wrong to him, it hurts."

Fred didn't upset her the way Bill had. You felt that Fred understood you, even if he didn't agree with you.

"You wouldn't want Bill to be a yes man, would you, Sandy? You couldn't admire him if he agreed with you when he thought you were wrong. Bill's a fine boy. He's honest. He's got to say what he thinks. You've got to understand him."

"Well, he's got to understand me too. I can't have someone preaching sermons to me about what's right and what's wrong."

"Sit down, Sandy. I want to tell you something," Fred said in his gentle way.

She sat down on the edge of one of the big club chairs, wondering what more there was to say.

"Sandy, many years ago I came East to study sculpture with a famous man named Johansson. He was one of the finest sculptors in the world, and I was fortunate enough to become his private secretary and student for over four years."

Sandy listened intently as Fred went on. "I lived with Johansson in his studio, worked with him, met the brilliant and famous people who came to see him. I learned a great deal from him. I could have learned a lot more."

Fred perched on the arm of the chair opposite Sandy.

"One day I quarreled with Johansson. It wasn't a big quarrel. It wasn't even about anything important. He blamed me for something I hadn't done. I was terribly proud and very stubborn. So I just walked out on him."

"You walked out!"

Fred nodded. "I packed the few things I owned and walked out. I never went back. I never heard from Johansson again. For a few years I did pot-boiling sculpture. Made molds for factories and jewelers. Nothing you could even call art. Johansson had told me many times that I had talent. But I threw it away over a small quarrel. When I walked out on him, I lost my touch, Sandy. I never could seem to get it back. You see, I walked out on everything that was important to me. I lost it all because I was too proud to humble myself and keep it."

Sandy looked down at Blackie and Mona Lisa stretched out on the rug. Blackie blinked up at her. She knew now why Fred had brought her back here.

A quarrel. Not even an important quarrel. Fred had walked out and lost everything.

"You know what I'd do if I were you?" Fred asked.

"What?"

"I'd go to the telephone and call up that cowboy friend of ours. I'd ask him to come over here and pick me up."

She shook her head. "He wouldn't come back now."

"I think he would, Sandy."

"If I called him up, I wouldn't know what to say."

"Let your heart speak for you, Sandy. Then the words will come easily. When the heart speaks, the heart will answer too."

She paused for one moment, fighting back stubbornness and pride. Then she went to the telephone, planted her finger squarely on the letter C, and dialed the Peabodys' number.

His aunt answered first and then Bill came on.

"Hello," she said. "It's me."

"Sandy! It's you!" He sounded unusually excited for Bill. "I've been fine-combing this whole town for you. What did you run away for?"

"I—well, I lost my head, I guess. I'm over at Fred's. He picked me up while I was walking home."

"At Fred's. Well, why didn't you say so? You stay right there. I'm coming over after you. Don't you move from that spot now." He hung up before she could answer.

She put down the receiver and looked over at Fred. "He sounded worried," she said. "As if he was terribly afraid something had happened to me."

She felt an inrushing tide of all the good she thought she had lost. It all came back now. Gadabout and Lucky Lady and Fred and Bill. She was not going to lose them after all. They were here waiting for her. Fred had helped her to keep everything that mattered, all the most important things in her life.

She went over to him and looked into his face, that kindly face with the nice eyes and generous mouth.

"Fred," she said, "when would you like to start painting my picture?"

6

THERE had never been such a spring for Sandy. Spring and summer had always been her seasons. The bright, hot days of the sandlots, of practicing pitches against the old mattress Greg had hung for her on the back of the garage, of strutting across the field at New Sharon High and taking over her strategic position on the pitcher's plate, or climbing into a crowded bus with the laughing, shouting girls on the team and traveling to any other high school that would play them.

Spring was the time of year. You couldn't beat it. If you lived to be a million, you'd never run into anything more wonderful than that feeling that came to you when spring arrived.

This year spring outdid itself. It was like no spring Sandy had ever known before. No, wait! It was like other springs, only glorified. It was the cherry on top of a wonderful double-scoop hot-fudge pecan sundae. It was the bananas on one of Marlene's cream-filled cakes. It was the ice cream—two scoops—on top of a strawberry-rhubarb pie.

And it was all because of Bill.

No one had ever brought so much into anyone's life as Bill brought into Sandy's.

Their friendship continued to revolve as it had begun, around softball. It was the most natural thing in the world for Bill to "just happen by" again on Saturday afternoon while Sandy was umpiring a game for the Blue Devils and Supermen. The sandlot at the foot of Gardner Street was electric with excitement when Bill swung his long legs over the fence that ran along one side. The bases were loaded with two out and Red Fenton at bat. The piercing shrieks of small-boy voices filled the air.

"Come on, Red, let's make it a homer!"

"Watch out for my catcher's mitt. It's brand new," Red yelled to two members of his own team who were fighting over his mitt.

"Aw, stop the stalling and let's *play ball!*"

"There's the Vaquero," someone shouted. "There's Wyoming Bill."

Thirty pairs of legs raced toward the lanky figure on the fence. He was soon pulled down off his perch. "Show us that windup again, Bill. Give us some points on batting, will you?"

The rest of the afternoon was Bill's. The Blue Devils and the Supermen held him captive, making him share with them all he knew about softball. It was considerable. Sandy, watching from the sidelines, learned a thing or two herself.

Bill showed them how to hold the ball for a pitch. He went through the grip and release for a drop, a fast ball, incurve or outcurve.

"Mix your pitches up," he advised. "Don't try to strike every batter out. Save some of your pep for where you're going to need it the most."

Bill gave them tips that showed a practical knowledge of every position in the game.

When it came to batting, they made him grab a bat and show them.

"If you choke the bat," he explained, holding it far up and swinging with a short stroke, "you'll place the ball all right, but you won't hit it very far."

He showed them how to stand, not crouching, and with the legs not too far apart. "You've got to stand so you can look right straight on at the pitcher, and get a good look at the spot where the ball is coming through to you." He grabbed hold of Red Fenton, who was illustrating. "No, not like that. You look like a stiff-legged old man, Red. Straight but not stiff."

He showed them how to swing and bunt.

"You've got to be sure of yourself when you come up to bat." He rumpled Red's fiery hair. "This guy's got plenty of confidence. But that's not enough. You've got to have good form too. That's half your battle at the plate. The other is being able to follow the ball. Don't leap at it. Don't take a wild clout at it as if it were a punching bag. Just keep yourself loose and keep your eye on the ball instead of the pitcher. Wait for that ball and then swing!"

The Blue Devils and the Supermen were goggle-eyed with admiration. They tried to detain Bill.

"I've got to go. I'm having supper early tonight."

"Aw, he's got a date with his girl," Red said. "Let him alone."

"I've got a date, anyhow," Bill said good-naturedly. The crowd broke up and Bill walked up Gardner Street with Sandy.

"The kids are crazy about you," she said. "It's nice of you to give them all that attention."

"You've given them quite a bit of attention yourself."

"That's different," she said. "I belong here." Then, quickly, "I didn't mean that you don't belong."

"I know," he said. "I know what you mean." For a moment, there was all that wistfulness in his face again, the look Sandy had seen several times and the look she had come in a way to dread. It seemed to separate her from Bill. He seemed to leave her and go galloping across the miles to a place she had never been, a place she could only vaguely imagine. Wyoming. She tried to reach out to it, to snare it in her thoughts. She recalled movies she had seen of vast, rolling land with foothills in the distance. Ranches. Hollywood style with movie-type cowboys riding beautiful horses which she preferred to watch instead of the actors. There was always one street in these pictures, a Main Street with a bank, a post office, a hotel, a sheriff's headquarters, and a few houses. There was always a girl. A blond girl, the heroine, who was so saccharine in her gingham dress, with a cameo at her throat, that Sandy couldn't stand her.

This, then, was Wyoming to Sandy.

She wondered what Wyoming was to Bill. He would never talk about it, even when she tried to pump him.

He would only say, in answer to her questions, *"Out home?* Oh, out home it's nice."

Nice, she thought. But how nice? I want to know.

He walked with her to the back door of her house. "Could you take a minute to show me a few of those soft-ball grips you were demonstrating this afternoon?" she asked.

"Sure," he said.

They went around to where the mattress hung on the garage and Bill showed her his grip for the incurve and outcurve, for the drop and fast ball. He watched her practice, stopping to correct her form and give her a few additional tips on the releases.

"Bill!" It was Marlene's voice calling from the back porch. "Your aunt just called up. She said supper is waiting for you."

"Now how did she know I was here?" Bill asked Sandy as he turned to go.

"I wonder," Sandy replied.

"I almost forgot to tell you," he said. "You and I are going to a hoedown tonight."

"A what?"

"A party. My aunt and uncle's been invited and they invited me and I'm taking you."

"You are?"

"Sure. It's at Elsie Sherman's house. Elsie's got a big place and she's giving a lawn party."

Sandy walked slowly over to him. "Do you mind if I ask who Elsie Sherman is?"

"She's a friend of my aunt's. Just got married a little

while back. She's a lot of fun." He started to go but called back, "Be ready at seven-thirty sharp."

"Hey," she called. "Come back here."

"What? I'm in an awful hurry, Sandy."

"Has it occurred to you that this Elsie whoever-she-is might not want me?"

"Don't be silly. Elsie likes people. Lots of them."

"Suppose I said I didn't want to go."

He looked dismayed. Then, "You're just kidding. Now you hurry up and get ready."

"I haven't anything to wear to a party."

He laughed. "Where have I heard that before?" he said, laughing. "I'll pick you up at seven-thirty."

Sandy stood there, shaking her head and watching him run down the street toward the Peabody house. "Honestly," she said, "he's the limit. The very, very limit."

She took the back steps two at a time and hurled herself into the kitchen, letting the door slam noisily behind her.

"Marlene," she shouted, although Marlene was only a few feet away, taking a casserole of beef and noodles from the oven. "I'm going to a party. With Bill. Tonight at seven-thirty. It's at Elsie Sherman's, a friend of his aunt's, and we're all going. His aunt and uncle too. It's a lawn party."

Marlene, with the casserole in both hands, swung around. Sandy had given her all the information in one gulp in order to forestall the irritating inquisition that would surely have occurred if she had left out one detail. Marlene set down the casserole and eyed Sandy.

"What are you going to wear?" she asked.

"Oh, anything." Greg had come in to hear the last question and answer and Marlene took evident delight in repeating the surprising news to him.

"If it's a party," Marlene said, "you can't wear just anything. You can wear that sweet pink dress I bought you for Easter."

"I'd rather die," Sandy said. "I'd rather die than wear that pink-lemonade ballet dancer's costume."

"It's the only party dress that fits you. You can't wear a school dress or a sweater and skirt to Elsie Sherman's party."

"All right. I'll wear my frontier pants then. They're practically brand new. I'll go dressed as a cowgirl." She knew she would never be allowed to do this, but it was fun to tease Marlene.

"You'll do no such thing," Marlene said. "Pants to a party! Who ever heard of such a thing?"

"You did," Sandy said brightly. "Just now."

Marlene assumed what she considered her best motherly attitude. "Seems to me," she said, "Bill might have given you more notice. Who ever heard of asking a girl to a party on such short notice?" She started serving supper, at the same time calling to Ran to come down. Ran's shoes clattered on the stairs. When he burst in, he was brought up to date on the conversation. "And I say," Marlene finished the account, "that Bill should have given Sandy more notice."

"That's old-fashioned." For once Ran sided with Sandy. "I never give my girls much notice. If you do, it gives them too much time to think. When a woman thinks, she's got to change her mind. That's the way women are."

Marlene turned to Greg for support. "Greg, you always call up a girl in plenty of time, don't you? At least a few days ahead." Then, airily, "I'm sure I'd never accept such a short-notice invitation."

Greg did not smile as he answered, but while Marlene's back was turned he winked at Sandy. "You and I have got to face it, Marlene," he said. "We're the older generation. The young ones do things differently."

Marlene turned, saw the point, and the kitchen rang with laughter as they all joined in.

"Well, it's nice you're going, anyway," Marlene said.

She meant it. Marlene was beaming. Sandy thought, She sure must have been wishing for me to have a boy friend for a long, long time!

All during dinner Marlene talked about the party. The boys had to listen. She knew Elsie Sherman slightly. She was a pretty young woman and they had just bought a house out on Country Road. She gave interesting parties. Her brother had an orchestra of his own and there was always music and dancing.

"You'd think Marlene was the one who was invited," Ran said.

"I'm just awfully pleased for Sandy. I think we all should be. I'm so glad that at—" Marlene interrupted herself just in time. She had almost let the cat out of the bag. She had almost said, "I'm so glad that at last she's got a boy friend, that at last she's going to have some social life." Sandy knew. Marlene had been afraid for

Sandy. Sandy could almost feel her thinking, With no looks and too much weight and no style and that breezy, devil-may-care attitude, she could have done a lot worse than Wyoming Bill.

Sandy gulped her second piece of pie and pushed back her chair. "Well, I'll just go change into my other pants," she said.

"Sandy!" Sandy stopped dead in her tracks. She turned around. Marlene stood up. She was every inch a mother now.

"You are not going to wear pants to this party. Neither frontier pants nor any other kind. You're my sister, and the least I can do is to see that you're dressed properly for one of Elsie Sherman's parties."

"Every good dress I've got is too young-looking." Sandy wailed. "That ruffled stuff makes me feel like a kid."

Marlene's face grew unusually sympathetic. She looked at Sandy long and hard, and as she looked, the kitchen with all its familiar objects seemed to fade away. Even Ran and Greg seemed shut out. There were just the two sisters appraising each other.

She's really seeing me for the first time, Sandy thought. She's seeing the real me, instead of the family baby.

"All right," Marlene said with a new softness in her voice. "You don't have to wear the pink-lemonade ballet costume. You can wear one of my dresses, that blue one you've always admired, Sandy. It's a little large for me, but I think it will just about fit you."

7

MARLENE had said the party would be big and interesting and Bill had promised Sandy that it would be fun, but she had not expected that it would be this big and interesting or this much fun.

At first Sandy felt uncomfortable to be rubbing elbows with people older than herself. The few birthday and high-school parties she had attended had been confined to people her own age. This was the first adult party she had attended and, in spite of herself, she enjoyed it. That was because of Bill. She soon learned that you had to enjoy anything you did if you were with him.

Elsie Sherman greeted them as they crossed the lawn from their car.

"Hello, Bill," she said. "I see you've brought your girl." Then, to Sandy, "Have fun." Elsie turned, greeting some new guests, and with Bill's aunt and uncle safely settled down for a game of bridge on the screened porch, Bill and Sandy were on their own.

Bill caught Sandy's hand and ran with her to the back of the house where most of the fun was going on. In a natural setting of tall trees, a wide expanse of lawn had been cleared and mowed down so that it was smooth and even as a carpet. Against the wall of evergreens stood a raised platform on which Elsie Sherman's brother had placed his band. Sandy knew about Toot Westcott's Troubadours. If you read the *New Sharon News* you often saw, at the end of the description of a party on the social page, "Music by Toot Westcott's Troubadours." They could play either society or country dance music and, with a change of costume, they were equally at home playing for a school dance or at the country club.

Tonight they had donned checked shirts and blue dungarees and clapped ten-gallon hats on their heads. They were playing "Camptown Races" and a lively square dance was already in progress, with Mr. Sherman calling the figures.

"Come on, let's join the fun," Bill said.

Sandy was glad it was a square-dance party. She had dreaded the dancing part of the affair, thinking it would be one of those stilted evenings where you had to dance with a lot of boys you didn't know and wouldn't like if you did know them. Once Ellie Winchester had dragged her to such a dance at high school and Sandy had had a miserable time, even though it was a tramp dance and she had been able to wear her old clothes.

This was different. This was all right. She could dance these country dances with the best of them. She had learned the steps and figures a long time ago, so long that she could not remember when, down in the sandlot on Gardner Street. On summer evenings when there was nothing else to do and they were tired of playing ball and no one would take them to the beach, they would get old Patsy Domenico to bring out his accordion and young Patsy Domenico to bring out his harmonica and they'd round up as many kids as they could and dance. There had been no moonlight-and-roses romance about their dancing. It had been just rough-and-tumble good fun. You danced the way you played softball, with all the energy and vigor you had.

Sandy's dancing tonight still had on it the stamp of the Gardner Street sandlot. In its zest and uninhibitedness it harked back to its rowdy-dow beginnings. She put everything she had into it. Forgetting that she was at Elsie Sherman's lawn party and dancing to Toot Westcott's music, she let her feet fly through the swing, the circle, the allemande left and allemande right, the grand right and left, with un-self-conscious abandon. She could almost hear Patsy Domenico's accordion and Patsy Junior's harmonica. She could almost feel the dust fly up around her down at the sandlot, and she blinked her eyes against it and clamped her mouth closed so as not to get a swallow of it.

She knew all the figures and steps. She could do a ladies chain or a do-si-do with her eyes shut. She knew how to slide on the chassé and hold her head up and back for the promenade. These were things deep inside her that she had learned on her own native soil, on her sandlot.

Without realizing it at first, she was drawing a lot of attention to herself. Then she became aware of it. The young men and boys wanted to join the set that she was in. They would lead their girls by the hand to Bill's and Sandy's side and say, "Mind if we join you?"

There was even a bit of scrapping over this. Since a set could accommodate only four couples, when two arrived at the same time to join the three couples already there, the boys started scrapping over which couple should stay.

Sandy was gradually aware that all the masculine eyes in their set were on her, watching her feet move. She noticed that when, in the quick-changing patterns of the square dance, a boy found himself dancing with her, he gained a certain liveliness he did not seem to have had before.

"Say, that girl of yours is some dancer," one of the boys shouted to Bill. "Where did you find her?"

"Oh, I brought her in from the West with me," Bill drawled to the questioner. The boy's mouth dropped open as he swallowed Bill's joke, and Sandy and Bill, laughing as hard as they could, went running off together for a cold drink.

Bill, gulping down his punch, stared at her. "How'd you get to dance so well?" he asked.

So she told him about the sandlot and summer evenings and the two Domenicos.

Bill shook his head. "Never underestimate the power of a sandlot," he said, and Sandy laughed as he pulled her back for another dance.

They had a wonderful time. They were the most popular couple in the place. All evening, people kept wanting to join their set; all evening the boys and men kept telling Bill what a good dancer Sandy was. Some of them even asked her to show them how to do the more difficult steps and for a while she was conducting an impromptu dancing class right there on Elsie Sherman's lawn to the tune of "Raggedy Ann" played by Toot Westcott's Troubadours.

They stayed to the very end, right down to the last dance when Toot Westcott played a few bars of "Goodnight Ladies" on his trumpet and shouted, "That's all!"

They did not even go then, because a jam session was proposed by those who had stayed this long and a small group of dancers moved down to the Sherman basement playroom to dance to the record player. Here Sandy found herself for the first time in Bill's arms, dancing to popular jazz. He discovered that she could do the Charleston, too, and they pounded out that dance together, doing it so well that the others cleared a space for them and stood by to watch.

Then, all at once, it was time to go. You couldn't hang on another moment without looking as if you expected to be asked to stay overnight! All the punch was gone, and all the sandwiches were eaten and there was no more cake, except a few crumbs which they scraped together and picked up in their fingers. The Shermans were smiling but obviously tired. So was everyone else. Everyone, that is, but Sandy and Bill.

They said goodnight and told Elsie Sherman they had had the best time in their lives, and they meant it. Then they rode home in the back of the Peabody's car and Bill held Sandy's hand. She did not mind. It seemed natural, not sloshy the way she had always thought such things looked.

When they pulled up in front of the Herzog house, Bill got out with Sandy and said to his folks, "I'll walk down to the house so as not to hold you up." So the Peabodys drove down to their garage and Bill and Sandy tiptoed around to the side of the house where a small hall light had been left burning for her.

Sandy looked up at Marlene's window and then over at Greg's. They were both open, and she knew that her brother and sister were already in bed. "I'm the last one home," she said softly to Bill, feeling elated by the thought that she had stayed out even later than Greg or Marlene. "I guess Marlene isn't worried as long as your aunt and uncle were there."

"Besides, she knows you're safe with me," Bill added. "I can always be depended on."

"Who's conceited?" she asked.

"I am," he said. "You told me so almost as soon as you met me." Sandy started to laugh, stifled it, and wound up giggling.

Bill backed her up against the house and put his hands against the clapboards just above her shoulders.

"I like you, Sandy."

"Why?" she wanted to know.

"There aren't any girls like you out home, Sandy. Out home there are a lot of things. Big things and beautiful. Things you can't talk about because it hurts so much remembering them and not having them. But no girls just like you."

"What kind of girl am I?"

"You're a lot of girls. You're the girl who plays softball as if her life depended on it. You're the girl who gets all soft when she looks at Lucky Lady and would break her neck just to ride her. You're the girl who can sit and talk with Fred and go down in the sandlot with the Blue Devils and Supermen, or dance so well that every boy at the party wishes he was with you. You're a lot of fun, Sandy."

"You forgot to mention my faults. I've got plenty of them. I get sore at umpires. Sometimes I'm fresh to Marlene. I make faces that aren't pretty. I eat too much. I get hurt easy."

"I like you anyway, Sandy." He dropped his hands on her shoulders. He did it so easily she could not pull away even if she wanted to because it seemed so natural.

"Sandy, when a boy has just been to a party with a girl he likes more than any other girl he's ever known, he wants to say good night a certain way."

"How?" she asked.

"Like this." Then, just as naturally as you would wind up your arm to release an incurve, Bill took her in his arms and kissed her.

When he let go of her she said, "Hey, you shouldn't have done that!"

He clapped his hand over her mouth. "Not so loud. You'll wake up your family." Then, grinning, "Sure I should have done it, and I'm going to do it again." He rumpled the top of her hair and whispered, "Good night, Belle of the Ball!"

8

THE day after Elsie Sherman's party, Fred telephoned and asked if Sandy would come out that afternoon for her first sitting. It was only to please Marlene that Sandy took along the blue dress she had worn the night before. Marlene insisted that Fred would want to paint Sandy in "something nice."

Sandy had other ideas about how Fred would want her to dress. During those evenings in the little caretaker's house on the Barton estate, Sandy had picked up, by exposure, something of the talk and philosophy and technique of artists. She knew that Fred would want to paint her as she really was, so she wore her frontier pants and a clean white shirt and tied her yellow rodeo neckerchief around her throat.

Fred was waiting for them when Bill and Sandy turned their bicycles into the parking space near the stables. They had ridden their bikes today because the Peabodys wanted to drive out into the country to see some friends. Fred pointed to Greg's suitcase strapped to the basket in front of Bill's bicycle.

"What's all this?" he wanted to know.

Sandy opened the suitcase and held up the blue dress.

"Marlene said you'd want to paint me in something nice, so I brought this along."

Fred looked the dress over, then he turned and glanced at Sandy's pants and shirt. "I like you the way you are," he said.

So they left Bill to look after the horses and went into the studio. Sandy found being introduced to the mystery of having your picture painted was more interesting than she had thought it would be. Fred let her watch while he mixed his colors, using a huge piece of window glass for a palette. Her eyes eagerly followed the bright splashes of color as Fred squeezed them from the tubes and the various off-shades which he mixed from them. She was fascinated by the number of brushes.

"I thought you used just one," she said, running her fingers across the handles of the brushes, from the merest speck of bristle to those an inch wide.

Fred had to fuss around until his easel was at just the right angle, and then there was more fussing as he posed her. She would stand up, holding a riding crop. No, that looked affected. She would sit down, on that bench, and he could dub in a stone wall later on, with a background of trees and bushes. He preferred to paint her against an outdoor setting. She was that kind of girl.

Did you paint everyone against a different backbround? she wanted to know. When Fred said yes, that was the only way to do a portrait, she asked how he would paint Bill.

As Fred made his first strokes across the canvas, he answered musingly, "With lots of space around him.

Bill needs space. He's hungry for it right now. You can see the longing in his eyes."

Sandy sat very still. She was thinking about what Fred had just said. Bill needed space. He was hungry for it, longing for Wyoming.

"Then you think Bill's not happy here," she said.

"I wouldn't put it so strongly. Homesick, yes. But not unhappy. You've helped to make him happy, Sandy."

"Me?" She forgot herself and turned around. Fred stopped painting. "How have I helped?"

"By giving him a friend. A boy can't be unhappy when he has a real friend."

The afternoon was not so tedious as Sandy had expected it would be. Fred talked with her about horses, and recalled some of his boyhood in a small Midwestern town. He told her about the climate out there, the extremely hot summers and cold winters.

"The first year I came East," he said, "I didn't wear an overcoat all winter." With his eyes on his canvas, he went on. "We had real snowstorms there. Here, when you get a few inches of snow, you call it a blizzard. We had to shovel all winter long."

Summers he had spent on a farm, and that was where he had learned to handle horses. He'd ridden a lot when a boy. Now he couldn't ride because of his leg. It was the first time he had referred to his lameness and he merely touched on the subject, passing over it quickly, as if he wanted no special sympathy.

So Fred had not always been lame. Sandy now had the

answer to the question she had wanted to ask Bill the first time she had met Fred. She had long since forgotten that question. Most of the time she even forgot Fred's lameness. She didn't think about it even when she was with him. She thought only of the interesting things he talked about, the gentle way he treated everyone.

So the afternoon passed. Sandy was permitted to stop now and then for a rest. Fred would offer her a cold drink and she would sit down again and he would get to work. Then, finally, he said, "I guess we'll quit for good now."

"You mean the picture is all finished?" she asked.

"Not by a long shot. A picture isn't painted in one day."

"Oh," she said, disappointed, "then I can't look."

"You can if you won't expect too much." She came and stood back of Fred.

"Is that me?" she asked, looking at the roughly outlined portrait. There was a shock of unruly hair combed in a high pompadour and chopped off abruptly at the ends. There were two eyes, grayish-blue. There was a nose that turned up and a pointed chin. Some yellow daubs at the throat were evidently going to be her neckerchief, and she could see the pointed collar of her white shirt where it lay open at her throat.

"Is that really me?" she repeated.

"Not yet. That's just any girl with a pointed chin and a retroussé nose, but if we work hard enough, we'll make it you."

"What's a retroussé nose?" she wanted to know.

"One that turns up a little."

"Is that bad?" she asked.

"Nothing in a face is actually good or bad, Sandy, until you put a person behind it. It's the thoughts, the feelings, that make a face what it is."

"Then maybe I can be good-looking someday?" she asked. "Not good-looking the way Marlene is, but in my own way."

He took hold of her chin. "You're very attractive already, Sandy. In your own way."

"How you look to people is important, isn't it?" she said. "I mean dressing right is important and being neat and so forth."

"It helps with the outside world," Fred replied.

"You mean if a girl is pretty like Marlene, she gets along better. She's bound to have lots of friends."

"No, I don't mean that at all." He was busy, scraping all the leftover paint to one side of his palette in a giant blob. "I mean that women have a powerful place in the world. A much more powerful place in many ways than men have, Sandy. Take you and Bill, for instance. Bill needs you. He needs your understanding and affection and tenderness—all the womanly qualities you have to offer. He has boys who are friends, but that's not enough. He's picked you because he wants a friend who's a girl. He wants you to act like a girl, to talk like one and dress like one."

"But you wanted me to pose in my frontier pants today!"

"Yes, because that's you now, Sandy. Someday we'll

do you in a dress. Not the blue one you brought today, because it doesn't belong to you and it doesn't look like you. Someday when you're wearing the kind of dress I'd like to see you wear, we'll paint you in it."

She would like to have gone on with this conversation about what she was and what she might be someday, but Fred wanted to get out to the stables to see how Bill was coming along.

"Besides, we've got a surprise for you."

"What?" she asked. "Tell me."

"If I told you, it wouldn't be a surprise any longer."

Bill had just brought Glamour Girl in from a ride. He called, "Hi. How did it go?"

"Practically painless," Sandy answered. "Almost as easy as going to the dentist."

"She's a good subject," Fred said. "She doesn't tighten up."

Bill was busy with his gear. He had the cowboy's love for his saddle. The way he handled it, you would think it was a pet animal instead of so much inanimate leather and metal. Sandy supposed he was getting ready to hang up his gear, so she was surprised when he dropped it against the wall. He turned to look at Fred and an understanding smile passed between them. Although Fred did not move his head, it seemed almost as if he nodded to Bill with his eyes.

Bill went over to Lucky Lady and led her out of the stall. He held her by the lead rope, making no move to reach for his bridle. He looked again toward Fred as much as to say, "The next move is yours."

Fred took down a bridle and held it out. "All right, Sandy," he said. "Tack her up."

"Who, me?" she gasped. "You mean tack up the Lady?" Fred nodded, holding out the bridle to her. She went slowly over.

He's going to let me ride the Lady! she thought. That's the surprise. At last he's going to let me ride her!

Her hands trembled as she took the bridle. Fred held on to it, looking deep into Sandy's eyes. She saw something in his expression that quieted the churning inside her and steadied her hands. It was as if Fred were saying, "I believe in you, Sandy. I know you can ride Lucky Lady and that's why I'm letting you do it."

What he actually said was, "Remember, she's a fool about her head. So take it easy."

Sandy glanced over at the Lady. She was snuffing the rope, already fighting before there was anything to be alarmed about. That sixth sense of hers which made her the high-strung, sensitive horse that she was was now warning her that something unusual was about to take place.

Sandy was not afraid of Lucky Lady's shenanigans. Her own initial excitement had given way and she had only one thought on her mind. *She was going to ride the Lady.* With the bridle in one hand, she fished in the pocket of her pants with the other, easing out a few pieces of carrot which she had brought along for Gadabout. She went slowly toward the Lady, head on. She knew this was not the way to approach a head-shy horse. She had seen Bill bridle the Lady many times, and he did it with speedy skill from the side, seeming to come up to her from nowhere and slip the bridle over her head before she realized he was nearby.

But Sandy had pitched too many softball games in her own unique style to believe that the only way to get results was by imitating someone else. She had a strong aversion to handling the Lady in Bill's way, by making her believe he wasn't there. Sandy and the Lady were going to be friends for a long, long time. She was going to ride her not only today but other days. She was not going to have any trickery or deception between them. She loved the Lady too much for that.

Trickery was based on fear, the fear that you couldn't trust someone. All this head-shy business was plain panic. Someone long ago had frightened the Lady and no one had taken the trouble to break that habit of fear. Everyone who handled her had said, "She's a hard horse to handle. She's a fool about her head." They had strengthened the Lady's jitters by giving in to them.

Sandy was aware that someone was talking to her. She heard the words, sharp and commanding, but she was not sure whether the voice was Bill's or Fred's.

"Watch out. Don't approach her head on!"

She kept going, slowly but positively, progressing toward the restless Lady. The horse snuffed the rope but when Sandy held out her hand with the bits of carrot, the Lady sniffed. She hesitated, then reached out to accept the proffered treat.

Sandy talked to her. "Hello, Lady," she said. "You and I are going to be friends. You're not afraid of me and I'm not afraid of you. I like you and you'll like me after you know me. Now let's not have any nonsense about that silly old head of yours."

She paused. For a moment, a wave of uncertainty swept over her. Once the carrots were gone, Lucky Lady might start acting up again. This was a test as much for Sandy as for the horse. If Lucky Lady started pitching about so she couldn't bridle her, Sandy might not get another chance. She had broken all rules so far in her handling of the horse, and Fred might not dare to let her try it again.

The Lady finished her carrots and sniffed for more. She looked at Sandy. Her ears went back and for a moment it appeared that she intended to give trouble. But she didn't. She was listening to Sandy's voice.

"I'm going to put your bridle on now," Sandy said, her voice sounding a lot more confident than she felt. "I don't want any nonsense about it, Lady. You're to hold still and let me do it."

Then with a swift, sure movement, she slipped the bridle over the Lady's head. Straight on, face to face, eye to eye, the horse and the girl looked at each other.

Lucky Lady snuffed the rope once or twice, just as if to say, "I can't back down altogether. I can't be a push-over." Then she stood perfectly still, sniffing the air. Sandy held out another piece of carrot and the Lady gobbled it up.

The saddling was easier, because the Lady held still. Sandy used the same technique as she had for the bridle, making her movements deliberate and aboveboard. No deception, no guile. She spoke to the horse as she worked, letting the Lady know what she intended to do and telling her that she expected to get some cooperation. Sandy felt the girth to be sure it was properly adjusted and then she turned to Bill.

"Give me a leg up, will you?" she said.

He cupped his hands and she swung onto the horse's back. The Lady's ears went back and she started to pitch. Sandy leaned over and stroked her neck. "None of that," she said softly. "There's no reason to pitch. You and I like each other. What's all the fuss about?" The pitching stopped as abruptly as the rope-snuffing had a few moments before.

Sandy leaned over and kept talking to the Lady, encouraging her. "You're a good horse," she said. "You're a Lady. That's your name and from now on you're going to act like one."

It was only then that, as Sandy straightened up, she became aware of her audience. Fred and Bill were standing there watching her. She glanced from one to the other. Bill's mouth was wide open and he stared, speechless and amazed, as if he had seen a ghost.

Fred was more articulate. He was excited. Sandy could tell from the spots of color in his cheeks and the brightness of his eyes. She had never seen him look quite like this before.

"Well, I'll be darned," he said. "I wouldn't have believed you could do it," he muttered, shaking his head. "I honestly would never believe it if I hadn't seen it with my own eyes."

9

IT WAS only a matter of days before Lucky Lady became known as Sandy's horse. Fred was the first to admit it.

"Yes sir," he would say whenever Sandy came over to the Barton estate, "she's all yours. A one-man horse, that's what she is. Not the first time I've seen such a thing happen. How about it, Bill? You've known a few ponies from the rough string out home who took a special shine to one waddy. Meek as a lamb for the one they love."

Bill had to agree, although he was not so joyfully articulate about the admission as Fred. It was true, he said, that Sandy and Lucky Lady seemed to have reached an understanding. There could be any number of reasons for it. With pitching horses like the Lady, sometimes a woman's hand was best. They liked the gentler touch. Maybe the suddenness of Sandy's approach that first day had turned the trick. Everyone else had been showing so much respect for the Lady's feelings, and Sandy just walked right up and laid down the law to her.

"Anyhow," he said, "we'll have to rename her, I guess."

He explained that out home, whenever a horse deserved a new name because of his unusual actions, he was given one. "So I guess we better call the Lady something else now. How about 'Love That Gal?' " As far as Bill was concerned, the Lady was Love That Gal from then on.

Sandy was not surprised at the affection Lucky Lady showed for her. She had known all along, from the first time she had seen the horse, that someday it would have to be this way. You couldn't love an animal the way she loved the Lady and not get some response.

"We speak the same language," was her laconic reply whenever Fred or Bill brought the subject up.

It was true; they did. Every evening Sandy rode the Lady. On the afternoons when she was not practicing or playing softball, she would ride out on her bicycle to the Barton estate after school was over. More often than not Bill joined her, pedaling his bike beside hers along the dirt road that led to the estate. While he busied himself at the stables, Sandy would go over to the studio to sit for an hour or so while Fred worked on her portrait. Sometimes they rode their bicycles back to the Herzog house for a quick snack and then they would borrow the Peabody car and return to the estate for their evening ride.

Several times they were invited by Fred to "try pot luck" at his own table. Fred was quite a cook, and having supper at his place was almost as good as having a party. He had special dishes he had learned to cook here and there, in all the knocking about he had done. He knew how to prepare spaghetti and meatballs and chicken *cacciatore* in the Italian style. With these dishes he would serve nothing but Italian bread from the Renzulli bakery, and the dessert had to be cheese and fruit.

Fred was a stickler for "making things hang together." If he served baked beans, they had to be done in a big crock he had picked up in an antique shop and the brown bread must be Boston style; nothing else would do.

Fred liked to entertain with a lavish hand. He would pile their plates so full that even Sandy, who was no slouch at the table, would shout, "Enough. Please, Fred, no more!"

He kept his refrigerator stacked with food, jammed full, and he liked to throw open the door and show off its contents. A pile of steaks, frozen chickens, two half-gallon containers of ice cream, jars of pickles and olives, pies, plenty of bacon and eggs were only a few of the things he never let himself run out of.

"I was hungry once," Fred explained. "For a long time. I swore if I ever got on easy street again, I'd never run out of food."

"You sure won't," Sandy told him. "Not you." Fred laughed, pleased as could be.

There were other things besides plenty of good food at Fred's place. During the afternoons when Sandy posed for her picture, Fred always kept up a running conversation while he painted. Without consciously trying, Sandy was learning a lot from Fred. He was that kind of person—you could not be around him without learning.

In two afternoons of posing, she learned more about color than Marlene and all her clothes-conscious friends knew. She learned, for instance, that you tried for an arrangement involving red, yellow, and blue, if you wanted a completely harmonious color scheme. Fred flipped the pages of magazines, pointing out advertisements in color to show what he meant.

"Some of these are pretty crude," he said. "Wait, here's a good one. The yellow is chartreuse and the red is a shade of coral and the blue just the palest suggestion of mist in the background."

She sat there making up color combinations while he painted her and then she recited them to Fred for his approval or correction. Suddenly she burst out laughing. "Wait till Marlene gets dolled up for her next date. Will I be able to tell her a thing or two!"

"Charity begins at home," Fred replied.

"You mean I ought to dress better myself?"

"I'd say there was some room for improvement," Fred answered with his usual honesty.

"Even if I bothered to fix myself up, who'd give me a second look?" she snorted.

"Lots of people would." Fred stepped back to look at her portrait, then touched up some spots here and there. He finally came over and turned her head just a little. "But you've got to do a real job on this dressing-up business, Sandy. Most women don't study themselves enough. Take that blue dress Marlene wanted you to wear for your portrait. The color was wrong for you. You should never wear that shade of blue, no matter how much you like it."

She asked the question without daring to move her head. "What color is right for me?"

"Off shades. Subtle colors. But they've got to be vibrant tones, or they won't do the job for you."

"Why?"

"Because if the color isn't able to hold its own, Sandy, you're going to dominate it. You're that kind of person."

"But I thought Marlene's blue dress was very pretty."

"Maybe it was all right for Marlene, but there was too much dress for you. You need simple things. The plainer the better, Sandy."

She learned other things from Fred, things that could not be filed away for future reference as easily as the information about color and line and form, but which were in their own way even more enlightening.

She would get Fred to talk about the years he had spent with Johansson, about his life in the great man's studio, the people who visited there. The names were glittering and impressive, for most of the great people of Johansson's era had found their way to his door. Fred was a graphic storyteller. Sandy could visualize scene after scene being enacted as Fred talked about Johansson and his friends. Sandy listened carefully to what these people talked about. Her ears were wide open for their phrases of speech as Fred repeated almost verbatim the conversations he had overheard. Sandy absorbed the atmosphere of this realm of artists and statesmen and journalists and stage people and bankers and poets through every pore, reaching out hungrily to a world that was so far removed from Gardner Street. Gardner Street! Where the Herzogs and their neighbors had no other thoughts than their dinner or their supper, their television sets, and rides in their cars, and whether to paint their houses white or gray next spring.

So, under Fred's watchful and affectionate eye, Sandy took on a new something and began to bloom. Fred himself joked about it. "Sandy's blooming," he said one day to Bill. She's bursting out all over, and I don't mean she's putting on weight. In fact, I think she's lost a little."

"You're my friend for life," Sandy told him.

Whatever it was, other people noticed it too. At school she tried toning down a little. She discovered that you could make someone hear you just as well if you spoke in a normal tone of voice instead of shouting yourself hoarse. Instead of dashing pell-mell through the corridors at school, whamming into everyone and everything in sight, she tried walking for a change. "Something's wrong," her schoolmates cackled. "Sandy hasn't been given a detention for running through the halls all week!"

When she took some of the raggedness out of her hair-do and let the ends curl up naturally and coaxed the high pompadour into a wave instead of giving it the appearance of an abandoned bird's nest, the girls approved. "You look a lot better," they told her. "Better use some lipstick, too. It won't contaminate you."

So she did. She tried it alone in her room, having borrowed a discarded lipstick from Marlene's dressing-table drawer. It felt unpleasant at first.

"Ugh!" she said to her reflection. "What goo!" But she left it on, and in a short time she became so used to it that she forgot about it.

"Why, it looks good!" Marlene exclaimed when Sandy,

the lipstick still on, walked into the kitchen. "Only you need a lighter shade."

"I'll ask Fred about that," Sandy said.

"Fred!" Marlene snapped. "You'd think Fred knew everything about everything."

"He does," Sandy answered. "Why don't you ask him over to supper some night so you can see for yourself? He's swell."

"All right, I will."

Marlene was as good as her word. She invited Fred over before the week was out. The whole family met him. Bill was asked for supper too, to make Fred feel at home. Everyone liked Fred. Ran summed it up for the whole family after Fred had driven off in his old car, with all the Herzogs standing there and pleading with him to come back again soon.

"He's a regular guy," Ran said. "He's real."

10

THE softball team were having the time of their lives. Sandy had always been their center of attraction, the girl who could pitch a winning game and furnish enough laughs to make the bus trip to and from another school a hilarious event. Sandy, the old Sandy with the tangled hair-do and funny faces and noisy talk and quick-on-the-trigger answers, was a barrel of fun.

The new Sandy who fluffed up her pompadour and used lipstick, who was having her portrait painted by a real artist and who practically owned a horse named Lucky Lady, the Sandy who had a crush on Wyoming Bill, was more fun than a barrel of monkeys.

There were some who said she was getting spoiled, but they were the catty ones who resented the now apparent fact that Sandy was a very attractive girl. Most of the girls liked her even better than before. She was deepening, they said, now that she had other things to talk about besides softball. On a bus trip she could still be lighthearted, with her quips and grimaces and humorous banter. But she could have her serious moments too. A girl could talk to her about a date these days, and Sandy would listen sympathetically. A girl could ask her about a new dress or a new lipstick and get a civil answer. Sandy had even gone down to Bemberg's with Ellie Winchester to help her pick out the orchid dress Ellie planned to wear to the Senior Prom. In only one thing did Sandy remain unchangeable, and that was her determination to pitch the best game of softball in the county.

The New Sharon softball team played Westbrook away. It was a bright, cool day, the kind of weather when the girls considered themselves mighty lucky to be getting out of school a whole hour early to climb into a bus, even a rattling old jalopy of a bus that hurtled them almost to the ceiling at every bump. On the ride over, they chatted about the Starlight Dance that would be held at the outdoor dance floor of the Longbeach Club. It was sponsored by the General Organization of the school and was intended as a substitute social event for those who could not attend the Senior Prom. Sandy, who had little expectation of going to either the Prom or the Starlight Dance, sat well at the back of the bus and watched the road behind them.

Bill was on his way to Westbrook too, with the boys' baseball team, for which he was acting as official scorer. Sandy's watchfulness was finally rewarded as the boys caught up with them. The baseball team was traveling in four cars and Bill was jammed into the rumble seat of the last one with two other boys. He spied Sandy and waved. Then his car sped past the girls' bus, honking until it was lost from sight.

Westbrook was a small school with plenty of spirit and they usually played a good game. Today the Westbrook girls had just received their class books and they were huddled in groups on the grass, exclaiming and laughing over the remarks in the Class Prophecy, the Class Will, the Roll Call.

Sandy glanced from the girls to the umpire for the day. He was a stocky man in his late thirties who looked as if he could play a good game of ball himself. He seemed friendly enough, but there was something so efficient in the way he yanked his umpire's cap over his eyes and checked the scoring tabulator in his left hand that you knew he would tolerate no nonsense.

Sandy and Dodo warmed up. Without seeming to be aware of anything but the ball that went back and forth between them, Sandy was taking in the whole field. Westbrook had two pitchers, a nervous girl in blue shorts, a man's shirt, and a white visored cap, and the other a lean sporty-looking brunette in navy denims. The girl in the visored cap was chosen to pitch first, and Sandy, watching her warm up, saw that for all her jitters, she did have a good pitching arm.

Sandy was pleased to see Westbrook's increasing absorption in their new class books. That was all to the good. If you could keep Westbrook's attention on who had been voted the best-looking, the most popular, the most original in the class, you could certainly keep their minds off softball. A girls' team was excitable enough as it was without giving them all that dynamite before they got out on the field.

The umpire called, "Batter up!" and the game began. As the visiting team, New Sharon was up at bat at the top of the first. Sandy pushed her hands through her pompadour and hiked up her jeans as she waited her turn at bat. There was some cheering from the Westbrook rooters, a small group of girls and boys who had come out to watch their friends play. The New Sharon team urged its own girls on, calling, "You can do it, Pat. Nice try. Make it a hit this time."

But Pat Manero was struck out on a fly and Sandy stepped up to bat. She swung at the first pitch and missed it. "Strike!" the umpire called. The second was a ball. The third came at her like a cyclone and she mentally noted, "This pitcher is even better than I thought," as she swung and met it head on. It flew into the infield. The shortstop fumbled and Sandy got to first.

"Atta girl," her teammates shouted. "Nice work, Sandy."

Dodo came up next and was struck out as she hit and ran for first base, but Sandy managed to make it safe to second.

Midge Dubois was up next. A tall newcomer to the team, she had the reputation of being an excellent batter. Today she was a little uncertain, still feeling her way since this was her first appearance with the varsity, but she managed to make a hit on her third try and she went to first as Sandy went to third.

Wendy Mason, New Sharon's glamour-girl captain, was next. Sandy pressed her lips together and shook her head as Wendy stepped up to bat. The umpire could save some time by calling her out now before she even picked up the bat, for all the good she was. Everything about

Wendy irritated Sandy—her short-stepped mincing walk, the ultrafeminine carriage of her head and shoulders, the affected stance, the petulant facial expression.

"Strike!" the umpire called as Wendy swung at it.

"Strike two!"

"Might as well make it three strikes," Sandy mumbled to herself.

"Ball one," the umpire announced.

Oh, thrill, Sandy thought. We're going to prolong the agony.

"Ball two." Wendy grinned fatuously and got ready for the next pitch.

"Ball three."

For Pete's sake, Sandy thought. Has she got the pitcher hypnotized with her glamorous performance?

Sandy perked up, wondering which the next would be, a ball or a strike. She kept her eye on the ball and got on her mark. The pitcher was taking her time.

It's going to be a fast ball, Sandy thought. It may knock Wendy over, but it won't bring me home. She was so sure of this that, for a moment, when Wendy struck the ball head on, smacking it in the right spot, Sandy was dazed from shock. She recovered fast and started running. So did Midge and Wendy. From the yells of the New Sharon girls, the ball had gone far into the outfield. Sandy reached home, shook hands with Dodo and Pat and Ellie Winchester, and then wheeled around to watch the miracle. Wendy was running around the field. Correction! She was almost flying around the field and she slid—slid was the word for it, because she got down off that high horse of hers and slid home on her stomach just before the catcher tagged her.

"Safe," the umpire called.

The New Sharon girls grabbed hold of each other and jumped up and down in uncontrollable joy. "Three runs," they congratulated each other, "and one of them a homer."

Helen Ackerson was up next, and she was put out by a foul tip which was easily caught by Westbrook's catcher, but the New Sharon elation was undimmed as Westbrook went up to bat and Sandy walked to the pitcher's plate. Three runs in one inning was something to crow about, and Wendy Mason had done her share to make them possible. Commenting on it, Sandy said to Dodo, "It just goes to show that you can't judge a book or a glamour girl by the cover."

Sandy, on the pitcher's plate, was in perfect form this afternoon. She put out the first two Westbrook girls as fast as they came up to bat. The third girl had two strikes called against her, then fouled three times and finally made a fair infield hit and got to first base. The fourth girl went out on a fly. New Sharon cheered Sandy and Westbrook mumbled its displeasure.

"She can't pitch," they commented. "She's just lucky."

Sandy laughed. It was the price you paid for being good.

The next five innings were a pushover. Westbrook managed to score one run but New Sharon scored four more, making a total of seven. Two of them were made when Sandy sent a ball into the outfield, bringing a girl home from third and herself duplicating Wendy Mason's home run of the first inning.

Then two things happened that turned the tide of the game. Westbrook got wise and changed pitchers and New Sharon. . . . Well, it wasn't Sandy's fault really. It was just one of those things, just a bad break that came up so suddenly she wondered afterward how it ever happened.

The new Westbrook pitcher was a surprise to them all. Sleek and streamlined, she pitched the way she looked, and her pitches skidded through the air like greased lightning. Sandy sized her up in a minute. She was a short-term pitcher, the kind of girl you can put into a game only near the end when you want to boost the morale of your team. She wouldn't last. She would burn herself out fast, but while she was there she had literally plenty on the ball. And while she was in there pitching, the opposing team just did not stand a chance of hitting safely.

New Sharon went into the field at the bottom of the seventh inning with the score still 7–1. They had not been able to make any runs with this tall brunette releasing them so fast, but they were still far ahead. With Sandy in such good pitching form, they had nothing much to worry about. You might almost say the game was in the bag.

Then the big trouble really happened.

The first girl up at bat for Westbrook was the new pitcher. Sandy didn't know her real name. She had heard the girl's teammates calling this streamlined whiz with the jet-propelled pitch "Za-Za."

"All right, Za-Za," they would call out to her. "Make it a good one now." She stood with her long legs apart and her long arms swinging the bat with complete self-assurance.

"I will," she called back to her teammates. "I'll make it a good one." Sandy had never seen any girl on any softball field with greater poise or more self-confidence.

Dodo gave the signal for a low pitch and Sandy wound up. She used the windmill windup as Bill had taught it to her. When she let the ball go, it was a fast, hard pitch, low but not too low and Za-Za let it pass.

"Ball," the umpire called.

Sandy swung around. "Ball?"

"Too low," the umpire nodded.

Dodo beckoned to Sandy and walked slowly out toward the pitcher's plate to fulfill her mission of keeping the high-strung Sandy toned down. In her own quiet way, Dodo talked to Sandy.

"I'd have sworn it was a strike myself," she said, managing to put some salve and comfort into her voice, "but don't let it get you. Try it low again, but this time not quite so low as before, and make it an outcurve. I think that will do the trick."

Sandy wound up and delivered the ball. It was a perfect pitch, with just enough curve.

"Ball," the umpire called again. He yanked his cap down over his eyes with a positive gesture and glanced at the tabulator in his hand as he added, "Too far out."

Sandy wanted to swing around again and shout, "What do you mean, ball!" but she pressed her lips together.

She turned back toward the sleek Za-Za, and got ready for another pitch, but her hands were shaking. What was the matter with this umpire? Just like a man, the minute a pretty girl comes up to bat he has to get hypnotized. Sandy was torn between disgust and anger but she kept her emotions pretty well under control. She succeeded in putting the next ball right over the plate halfway between Za-Za's shoulder and knee. A man would have to be blind to call it anything but a strike.

"Strike!" the umpire conceded.

Sandy took her time. She would tease this good-looking Za-Za a little. Let her wait. When she was ready, Sandy let the ball go, another hard, fast one right over the plate. Za-Za swung and missed and again the umpire conceded a strike.

Sandy would make the next a clean-cut strike and the girl would be out. She wound up and delivered, making it a slow one for change of pace. Za-Za swung and clipped it hard, knocking it into the outfield near first. Shirley Somers caught it on the bounce. She threw it to first and Wendy Mason caught it long before Za-Za got there.

"She's out," Sandy yelled prematurely.

"Foul ball," the umpire called.

Sandy had swung around in time to see the ball roll past first base, within bounds. It was a fair ball, she was pretty sure, but she turned to her teammates for corroboration. Wendy Mason wouldn't commit herself, but Shirley Somers said it had looked like a fair ball to her, so she and Sandy spoke to the umpire about it.

He was impatient, eager to get on with a game that was

running into his dinner hour, so he dismissed the protest as unimportant.

"It looked like a foul from where I was standing," he said. Then he added what turned out to be the fateful remark of the game. "What the umpire says, goes."

Dodo, who had come up to listen in, muttered *sotto voce,* "It sure does. In Westbrook we not only have to lick the team, but the umpire too."

"What did you say, young lady?" the umpire called to her. Dodo stopped in her tracks and a flush of embarrassment crept up from her neck. The remark had not been intended for the umpire's ears. Dodo, of all the New Sharon team, would be the last one to be impertinent to a grownup or to show poor sportsmanship. Her comment had been a humorous quip intended to ease the strain of the situation, and certainly intended only for her own teammates' ears.

The umpire walked over to Dodo and took her by the arm. "I've a good mind to ask that you be taken out of the game," he said.

Dodo looked as if she were on the point of apologizing, but before she had a chance to say anything Sandy had pushed her way into the discussion. It made her boil to see poor innocent Dodo being bullied by a man twice her size.

"She wasn't talking to you," Sandy said. "She was talking to us girls. Haven't you got a sense of humor?"

The minute the words were out, Sandy realized she should never have said them. She didn't mean them to sound fresh, but somehow as the words tumbled out, they sounded almost insolent. Especially to a hungry man whose eye was on the clock and who wanted this game to be over in a hurry. He would not see a girl whose instinct was to protect one of her own teammates. He would only see a fresh pitcher who had spoken out of turn.

The irate man walked over to the two coaches and there was quite a lot of talk. Finally, Miss MacDonald motioned Sandy off the field and sent Pat Manero in to pitch. Miss MacDonald didn't even send Sandy in to play shortstop or left field as she often did when she relieved her as pitcher.

Sandy slumped down on the bench. She did not heckle the umpire. She did not even complain to the girls around her. She felt completely frustrated, but she kept it to herself and watched the game in silence.

It was a terrible game to watch. Everything went wrong from then on. Pat pitched as if she had never held a baseball before. Sandy had never seen her so bad. The fracas with the umpire had upset her, as it had the whole team. The inning dragged on and on. Pat walked four players. She threw pitches that even a ten-year-old, blindfolded, could have hit.

The game ended at last with a score of 7–6 in favor of New Sharon. It was a miracle that Westbrook didn't win. If it had not been for the partial distraction over the new class books, they might have won. Certainly it was no fault of Pat's that they were not able to make many more runs.

Pat cried on the way home, blaming herself for the way the game had fizzed out. The rest of the girls tried to console her. They told her it wasn't her fault. Some of them went even further than that.

"If it hadn't been for that fresh remark of Sandy's," Wendy Mason said airily, "asking the umpire if he didn't have a sense of humor, you wouldn't have had to pitch. I wish Sandy would stop being so quick on the trigger. It only makes trouble for everyone." Someone gave Wendy a nudge or she might have said more.

Sandy tried not to let it bother her. Just because Wendy had made one home run, the only one she had hit all season, she thought she was the star player of the team.

Dodo stuck by Sandy. She sat next to her on the quiet ride home. "Umpires are a funny lot," Dodo philosophized. "You never know what kind you're going to run into next."

Sandy did not answer. She was wondering what Bill would say when the story of today's game was relayed to him by the first busybody who could get his ear.

11

BILL was not moody as he had been the night they quarreled over the game with Brighthaven. He called for her at the usual time, his whistling, cheerful self. He ate a piece of pineapple upside-down cake saved for him by Marlene, and he was chatty and companionable on the way to the Barton estate.

Once there, Sandy had her first inkling that all was not well between them. Bill got down his own gear and led Lucky Lady from her stall.

"But I thought I was going to ride the Lady," she said.

"Fred's waiting for you. He wants you to pose for an hour while the light is still good."

"But you promised," she said. "You promised to take me out to Woodridge Glen tonight. It was a genuine, bona fide promise."

"Promises don't mean much nowadays," he replied. "I find that here in the East people don't take them seriously."

"What are you getting at?" she asked. "I never broke any promises to you."

"That's right. You never made any and you never broke any. Not to me."

"When did I ever break a promise to anyone?"

He went about the work of bridling Lucky Lady. Then, as he slipped his saddle on, he spoke. "Sandy, what happened at the game this afternoon? A lot of people have gone to the trouble of giving me some colorful accounts. I don't aim to jump to any conclusions. So please tell me yourself what happened."

"I was pitching a swell game until the last inning. We were six points ahead. Then Westbrook put in a relief pitcher. She held us down so we couldn't make any runs. When the new pitcher came up to bat at the bottom of the seventh, the umpire played favorites."

"Are you sure you're not just imagining it?"

"I'm sure he called them wrong, if that's what you mean. Strikes he called balls; a fair ball, foul. Dodo made one of her funny remarks under her breath. He overheard it and boy, did he get peeved! He started to bully Dodo. I merely asked him if he didn't have a sense of humor. The next thing I knew I was sitting on the benches."

"In plain words, you started another rhubarb, Sandy."

"I didn't start it, Bill. I finished it."

He stared at her, shaking his head. "Sandy when are you going to grow up?"

"If you mean get to be six feet tall like you, it just doesn't run in our family."

"You know what I mean. I don't mean size. I mean, when are you going to grow up and act your age?"

"I think I've been doing a pretty good job of acting my age, lately," she said. She was not disturbed by this argument. Tonight she was enjoying matching wits with Bill.

"I use lipstick. I've got a new hair-do. Lots of people even think I've got a boy friend. But sometimes I'm not so sure about that myself."

"See here, Sandy, if you think this is funny, I don't. Being your age isn't just putting on a lot of stuff from the outside." He turned away, busying himself with Lucky Lady, and plainly provoked by Sandy's flippancy.

"If you're so well informed about this growing-up business, why don't you tell me what it is?"

"Why bother to explain things to some one who thinks I'm a joke?" he said. "I don't like to be made fun of any more than anyone else does."

"I'm not making fun of you. I honestly want to know. If growing up isn't something you can see with your eyes, what is it?"

"It's an inside thing." He lapsed into his exaggerated drawl the way he did when he was thinking something through. "Out home when spring shows up, the grass comes to life. You see it waving red and gold and blue wherever you look. The cottonwood blows its white tufts over the ponds and you smell the poplars and the sagebrush and the pines. The mountains change color, from the shaggy, drab coats of winter to the shining blue and green and gold of spring and summer. You see the red buds of the ash and the purple cactus. You hear mountain streams rushing to go somewhere. And the coyote, never quiet, wails louder than ever. It's spring, you say. The land is shaking off the winter and waking up."

Bill kept his back to her, but she moved closer to him, pulled on by the earnestness of his words.

"But these are outward things, Sandy," he went on. "The things you see and smell and hear. Back of them, underneath them, down so far you can't get to it, is the force going on that makes all these things happen. It's inside the earth, under the sod, way below the grasses that wave across the land around our ranch. And even back of that, back of the roots that push up these growing things is a power no one could see no matter how far they dug. A power so big and important no piece of clod or earth could ever hold it."

He faced her, leaning back on his heels, cowboy fashion, resting against the Lady's flank. She saw in his face something she had never seen before. Suddenly for just that flash of a moment she saw the whole wide ranchlands of Wyoming, the vastness and the compelling solitude. The beauty, the freedom to move and be yourself, all the things Bill missed and longed for. The West was in Bill's face, shining in his eyes, reaching out to her, and she was able at last to walk across the barrier that had always seemed to separate them, to take his hand figuratively and walk "out home" with him.

"That power is the thing that makes you grow up, Sandy," he continued. "People call it different things. Some call it intelligence or experience or life. Some call it God. Whatever you call it, it's the thing that mellows people the way it mellows the earth. You ripen under it. You drop off the kid stuff. You don't have to shout so loud to be heard. You don't have to show off so much. You feel all quiet inside. You learn to think. It doesn't matter so much what other folks do or say because you're sure of yourself *inside*. You know who you are and where you're going. Like the mountain stream, rushing to go somewhere it's certain to reach. It doesn't have to whoop it up and try hard to go there. It just goes."

She didn't answer him. She looked down at the floor of the stables. Now that Bill's voice had grown quiet, there was silence in the place. She felt ashamed of her earlier flippancy. She wished now that she had not been so smart-alecky. Half of her was angry with Bill that he could make her feel this way; the other half admired him for being able to do it.

"If you don't mind," she said at last, "I think I'll go up and see Fred."

While she was posing for Fred, she was very quiet, quieter than she had ever been. Fred, always understanding, did not attempt to draw her into conversation. She was the one who finally spoke. "Fred."

"Yes?"

"Do you think I'll ever grow up?"

"You're growing up pretty fast these days, aren't you?"

"That's what I thought until tonight." Then she told him about this afternoon and her talk with Bill.

"Bill's right," she concluded. "All the time I've been sitting here I've been thinking about it. The outside things don't really count." Then, "Fred, some people never grow up, do they?" Fred nodded in agreement.

She went on. "Some people I know, people old enough to be my grandparents. I could name them off right here in this town, right on Gardner Street. Old people who've never really grown up."

Fred held the handle of one brush between his teeth while he reached for another. His eyes were on her portrait, but she knew he was listening and thinking along with her.

"After tonight," she said, "after what Bill told me, I'm afraid maybe I'll be like those people. I don't want to be like them, Fred. I want to be the kind of person Bill wants me to be. Deep, with lots of stuff *inside*. Not just a great big noisy windbag all my life."

Fred didn't laugh. She couldn't have stood it if he had. She was in earnest, dead earnest.

"There's just one thing Bill neglected to tell you, Sandy," Fred said at last.

"What's that?"

"That Wyoming spring he described doesn't come all in a moment. It's a gradual thing. It begins in little things, a root shooting up from the earth here, another one there, then a branch, a full-grown shrub, a flower. Then the whole shining panoply of spring." He dropped his brushes and, wiping his hands on a cloth, he came over to her. "You've begun, Sandy. Believe me, you've begun. And you'll go on and on. Because the real you is deep, the way Bill wants you to be." He took hold of her chin as if he were going to turn her face a little more toward the waning light, but instead he pulled it around so he could look into it.

"I believe in you, Sandy. I know what you've started to be and what you're going to be. All you need is the time and the space to grow."

12

BILL asked her to the Starlight Dance. He did it as casually as he did most things, pulling two tickets from his pocket the next evening and laying them down on the kitchen table.

"This one's for you, and this one's for me," he said. "So save a week from next Friday. Don't plan anything else."

It was that evening too that Bill gave Sandy her first lesson in jumping. He led Glamour Girl out and Sandy was told to put her gear on Gadabout.

"Can't I ride the Lady?" she asked.

"No, ma'am," Bill said with a finality that indicated no amount of coaxing or argument would win him over. "I don't even jump with the Lady myself."

He led the way through the bridle path to the northern boundary of the Barton estate where a row of fences of varying heights had been erected. They were old fences, in need of repair, and if anyone had ever used them for jumps, it must have been long ago.

"The important thing to remember about a jump," Bill explained, "is that Gadabout feels the same way as you. He wants to approach that fence smoothly, jump it safely, and land on the other side in his stride. Jump with him. Don't be just a passenger he's got to take over the fence. And stay up out of your saddle or you'll get left behind."

"You mean I might fall off?"

"No, I mean you'll flop back on your horse. That will make him drop his hind legs and rap the fence." Bill led Glamour Girl over to the lowest fence. "We'll try the low ones first," he said. "A jump over a low fence like this is just a very long canter-stride. Okay?" She nodded and watched him ride for the fence. There was nothing in Bill's action that betrayed any signals passing between him and Glamour Girl. Yet the horse approached the fence with her head up, her ears pricked. She was judging the height. Then she checked slightly and brought her hind legs forward. In the air, her head shot out, and her forelegs folded under so she would not hit the fence. One foreleg hit the ground before the other, then her hind legs landed and she cantered on.

Bill kept up out of the saddle throughout the jump. His hands were down. He tried it again and then again, calling instructions to Sandy.

"It's a matter of timing, Sandy. You have to know just when your horse will take off and judge the last few strides before the horse takes the fence. You try counting it while I do it."

She did, counting Glamour Girl's last three strides before the horse and Bill took off. "One—two—three, go!" Four times out of five Sandy struck the count right. Then

Bill let her try the lowest fence. He cantered along beside Gadabout, stopping short of the fence and encouraging Sandy to go over.

"That's it. Go along with him. Keep your hands up so he can use his head and neck. Give him rein!"

She felt Gadabout hesitate and put in an extra little stride. Then he went up and over. It was a thrilling experience, even better than socking a ball so hard into the outfield that you knew you had a homer. Bill cantered around and met her on the other side of the fence.

"Why did Gadabout take that extra little step?" she asked.

"Your timing was off."

"But I timed it perfectly almost every time you went over."

"You got excited and misjudged. Gadabout felt that excitement. He wasn't sure of you, and that's why he took that extra stride to save himself from rapping the fence."

"Did I do anything right?" she asked with a grimace.

"Sure; you didn't fall off. Don't look so worried. You were pretty good for a first try."

With this encouragement, she did better on the next jump and they practiced until the horses were bored and tired.

"It's really not difficult," she told Bill on their way back to the stables. "Why can't I jump with the Lady tomorrow?"

"No one jumps with the Lady. *No one.*"

"Why?"

"Because she won't have any part of it. The Lady doesn't want to jump."

"Have you tried her?"

"Several times. She just refused. Ran out on me. She's just running-scared of jumping, that's all. It's another sign of the bad training she's had."

"I could break that fear," Sandy said. "You said I'd never be able to ride her at first. You were wrong about that. She's not even head-shy with me. I bet she wouldn't be jump-shy, either."

"Jumping is different. No one jumps with the Lady."

She argued the question with Bill all the way back to the stables. At least she tried to argue, but Bill wouldn't answer her. When she pointed out that she had broken all rules with the Lady, that she could get her to do anything, and that even Fred conceded these points, Bill merely tightened the line of his jaw and clamped his mouth shut. It was clear that, as far as he was concerned, the subject was closed.

He took her out to the fences the next night and the next. They were using the higher hurdles now. The third night she was allowed to try them with Glamour Girl. Sandy could feel the difference between the two horses. Gadabout had been a quiet, routine jumper. It was just another job to him. Glamour Girl, on the other hand, acted like an actress before the curtain went up, all mettle and high spirits. Sandy felt the throb of anticipation every time she cantered up to a fence on Glamour Girl. This horse was harder to handle and Sandy had to be careful with the reins. Several times as they were going over, she felt herself about to be left behind. She grabbed hold of Glamour Girl's mane just in time to avoid jerking the horse's mouth. It was a big jump. It was always a big jump with Glamour Girl.

The next night Bill and Sandy went out to the fences, but Bill shook his head when he looked at the ground.

"The big rain last night has spoiled our fun." He jabbed the earth with a stick and brought up some mud. "You can't jump a horse in a muddy field. He might slip and go down."

They went back to the stables, got Lucky Lady for Sandy, and took their usual ride along the country roads. Sandy was happy to be on the Lady again. This was a horse! This was real riding.

"Her name sure is Love That Gal," Bill said.

Sandy ran her hand affectionately over Lucky Lady's neck. "She's the best horse in the world and I love her. Every time I ride her I tell her that." The Lady responded to the quiet stroking of her neck and shoulders. It seemed to calm her the way it always did.

I love you, Sandy thought as she leaned over the horse and felt the touch of the dark mane. You're the most beautiful horse in the world and I love you.

Then, straightening up, she thought, I know you'd jump for me. Even if you wouldn't jump for anyone else, you would for me. I'm sure of it.

13

SHE could not get it out of her mind. It became an obsession with her. All through the week end, she had one thought on her mind. She wanted to jump with the Lady.

On Sunday Fred called and asked if Sandy would come out to his studio for some work on her portrait. He said that Bill had to drive his aunt over to Brampton to meet the train on which his uncle was returning. If Sandy could get Greg to give her a lift out, Bill would stop at the studio later on and pick her up.

It was a beautiful day. The night before there had been scattered showers, just enough to leave the air with that clear freshness which was part of a perfect June day.

Sandy was quiet throughout the sitting. Fred painted with more absorption than usual. The portrait was almost finished. It looked like Sandy now, so much so that she wondered what there could possibly be left to do on it. Fred said it needed "polishing," so she sat patiently while he put the finishing touches on the painting.

She made a special effort to be cooperative today, because she had a favor to ask Fred. For that very reason it was hard to sit still. The favor she was going to ask kept pushing so hard against her that she wanted to jump up from the chair a dozen times and cry out, "Aren't you through yet?"

At last Fred threw down his brushes and started to scrape away the paint. "You were a good model today, Sandy," he said. "As good as any professional."

"I'll be sorry when the picture is finished," she said affably. "I've enjoyed doing it."

She got down off the little platform and went over to look at her portrait.

"It's good," she said. "I hope you'll let my family see it sometime."

"When it's all finished, we'll have a party and invite them."

"Fred." He looked up from cleaning his brushes. "Fred, can I ride the Lady this afternoon?"

"Bill will be here soon. You can both go out together."

"He may not get here for another hour. Even longer. And he might not feel like riding when he gets here."

"Bill not feel like riding!" Fred laughed. "That cowboy would rather ride than eat."

"It's Sunday and he'll be dressed up, and maybe he'll be tired after driving over to Brampton. It's a long way."

"Sandy, why do you want to ride the Lady alone?"

She avoided a direct answer. "You don't have to worry, Fred. She's very good with me. Better even than she is for Bill."

"Yes, I know. But we've made a sort of rule, you know. You're not supposed to ride without Bill. You know how Bill is about rules."

"But just this once won't hurt," she begged. "The Lady's used to me now."

She could see he was considering it. "Well, I suppose the Lady is as safe if you ride her alone as if you ride with Bill."

"I can handle her perfectly," she said. "The Lady and I understand each other."

"If I let you go alone, will you promise not to leave the grounds and to be back in half an hour?"

"I promise," she replied quickly. She would have promised almost anything if he had said she could ride the Lady alone.

"All right, but be careful." He went with her to the stables to see that she got off all right. She was impatient because he had to walk so slowly on account of his lame leg. Her impulse was to race ahead and be off. When she was ready to go, he came over to the door and stood there with a serious expression on his usually placid face.

"Be careful," he repeated. "And remember your promise, Sandy."

She walked the Lady over the bridle path for a few hundred yards or so, and then broke into a canter. She would keep her promise. She would not leave the estate and she would be back in half an hour. Fred had never thought of the fences. It had never occurred to him that she would try to jump with the Lady.

At a canter it took only a few minutes to reach the fences. Sandy led Lucky Lady up to the lowest one. For a moment she paused, remembering the showers of last night and recalling that Bill had warned against jumping a horse on muddy ground. She brushed the inner voice aside. They had been such light showers, with not much rain, hardly enough to make it worth mentioning. At least so it seemed in retrospect to Sandy, who wanted to believe this was true. She shrugged off the idea of testing the ground with a branch as Bill had done. That seemed unnecessary and overcautious.

She rode far enough back from the fence to get a good start. Then, before she broke into a canter, she leaned down and stroked the Lady's neck.

"We can do it," she said. "I know we can."

The Lady shook her dark mane and whinnied in response. Sandy started her off. Lucky Lady approached the fence and turned out long before she reached it. Sandy tried again. This time she leaned over and spoke to the horse as they drew near the fence. Her horsemanship was perfect. She had learned by now to calm her own excitement first. She knew how to stay up out of her saddle in the forward hand-gallop position. She was able to ride Gadabout and even the high-spirited Glamour Girl without being left behind. She knew enough to let the horse alone as it jumped and she could do that even with a bold, high jumper like Glamour Girl. Most important of all, she had learned to give the horse its head.

So she knew she was handling the Lady well.

This time the horse went closer to the fence. The Lady was alert, balanced, and when she checked slightly, bringing her hind legs forward and her head down, Sandy thought she intended to take the fence.

She did not. She swerved and ran around the jump.

Sandy tried it again, and again there was that proper approach as the Lady pricked up her ears and judged the height of the fence. She checked slightly as before. Sandy would have sworn she was getting ready to jump, but again the horse swerved and ran out.

Sandy whistled softly. "You're a smart one," she whispered close to the Lady's ear. "You act as if you're going to jump and then you run out. That's the neatest, most adroit refusal a horse can give. Where did you learn that sassy trick?"

Then, as they cantered back toward the starting point, she said, "All right, Lady. If you want to play cagy, I can play that game too."

She gave the horse the signal to start. This time she would not be fooled. She knew a refusal was coming and she got ready for it. As the Lady cantered toward the fence, Sandy went into it strongly, holding the Lady straight at it. She could feel the horse slowing up and coming back to her, so she squeezed strongly with her legs. The Lady whinnied. It was not the affectionate whinny she gave when her neck was stroked. This was a cry full of rebellion and anger and fear.

Sandy did not let it stop her. She held the horse straight at the fence, squeezing more strongly on the last three strides. The Lady checked, hesitated, but there was nothing for her to do but go over. Her head and neck reached out. She folded her forelegs under her.

Then it happened. Her hind legs slipped. Sandy could feel them slide on the wet ground and she felt also the frantic efforts of the Lady to regain her balance. The

Lady whinnied again. This time the cry was all fear. Sandy felt herself slipping as the horse struggled for a balanced landing. She grabbed for the Lady's mane but it was too late. She slid off and the heel of her shoe caught in the stirrup. She tried to wrench it free and couldn't.

The Lady cantered wildly on, dragging Sandy over the rough ground beyond the fences. Instinctively, Sandy put her arm up to protect her face. Instinctively, too, she called to the Lady, talking to her as calmly as she could, asking her to stop. The Lady did not stop at once. She dragged Sandy another twenty-five yards. Then suddenly she seemed to hear Sandy's voice for the first time through her own frenzied whinnies. She paused and swung around. Sandy saw her chance. She grabbed at a rock and held on.

"Don't move, Lady," she called. "Stand still. Be good and don't move."

The Lady stood still, pricking up her ears. Sandy lay there, wondering what to do next. From where she lay it was impossible to free herself from the stirrup. She could only hope that the Lady would not move, that she would not break into a canter and drag her across the rocky meadows of the estate.

The Lady sniffed the air. She turned her head and shook her mane and looked back to where Sandy lay clinging to the rock. Then she broke into a low whinny. She kept at it, letting the sound rise in volume so that it became almost a wail. It sent shivers through Sandy. It had an eerie quality like the signal of a wild horse calling to his herd, a distress signal rising to a crescendo of persistent pleading for someone to come and help.

Sandy lay there for what seemed hours. Her leg was numb. She tried to keep her head and shut out the desperate thoughts that pounded for admission. If she lay here much longer she might lose consciousness. Maybe no one would hear the Lady. They were far enough away from the road so that the Lady's cry of distress might not be heard. If any one did hear it, they might not bother to investigate. Even if they bothered, how could they hope to find Sandy in this wooded stretch barricaded by tall evergreens and tangled shrubbery?

Yet the distress call kept up. The Lady did not relent. Occasionally she would stop to prick up her ears and sniff the wind. Then she would begin again, low, the sound rising steadily and bursting at last into the piercing wail that sent shudders over Sandy.

Then, during one of the pauses between whinnies, Sandy heard a sound. Someone was coming. She heard the cracking of branches as someone pushed aside the shubbery to find them.

It was Fred. Walking as fast as he could, he limped into sight. When he saw Sandy lying there, the color drained from his face. He did not say a word, but stroked the Lady's neck to calm her. Next he went to the stirrup where Sandy's foot was caught. At first try, even Fred could not free her heel. The fall and the dragging had twisted her foot in the stirrup.

"Couldn't you just loosen the saddle?" she asked.

"I thought of that, but I don't dare. Not the way

your foot is caught in that stirrup. If the Lady got startled before we finished the job, she'd drag you with her."

He went patiently to work, giving her directions to move her leg this way and that, as he tried to free her foot. Sandy ground her teeth through the painful experiments but she did not cry out or whimper. The heel was loosened at last, and Fred bent over to help her to a sitting position. He tried her leg to make sure it was all right.

"No broken bones," he said. "You can get up as soon as you feel up to it." He helped her up. She was shaken but she limped around, trying to get rid of the numbness. They were so busy pulling her together, brushing her off and making sure there was no serious damage, that they did not see Bill. The Lady's whinny told them of his presence.

"What happened?" Bill called, running toward them. "Are you all right, Sandy?" He looked at her torn shirt, the bruises on her face and arms. Then he turned to Fred. "Are you sure she's all right?"

"No bones broken," Fred reassured him. "Only a bit battered and bruised. We can be mighty grateful."

"How did it happen?" Bill asked. He looked from Fred to Sandy. "Sandy, did you take the Lady out alone?"

"Fred gave me permission."

"What happened after you left the stables, Sandy?" Fred asked in his quiet way. "How did the Lady unseat you?"

She looked them both straight in the eye before she

answered. It was a hard thing to do, but she faced them.

"I jumped with her," she said. Her voice was steady as she told them but then her nerve failed her and she had to look away into the tangled bushes at her feet.

"You jumped with the Lady!" Bill cried out.

Fred came between them. "I thought you said the Lady wouldn't jump, Bill," he said.

"She wouldn't. Not for me, anyway."

"She refused at first," Sandy went on slowly, "but I got her to go over. It would have been a perfect jump if the ground had been dry. The Lady lost her balance and my foot caught in the stirrup when I slipped off."

She started the account bravely enough, but as she finished she became frightened at Bill's expression.

"You took the Lady out alone." His voice sounded grim, almost ominous. "Then you tried to jump her on muddy ground. When she had sense enough to refuse, you forced her. You've been jumping three days and to-day you forced a jump-shy horse over the fence on muddy ground."

He clenched his hands in anger, an anger which seemed even more intense because of the scare Sandy had given him.

"Do you realize what you've done?" He continued to clench and unclench his fists as if he wanted to grab hold of Sandy and shake her. "You took a horse that belongs to somebody else and deliberately exposed that horse to danger. The Lady might have been seriously injured. You might have been a whole lot more banged up than you are." His voice trembled with increasing anger.

"And as for Fred, he would have got the entire blame. He's responsible for this place and everything on it. He's one of the best friends you've got, and your selfishness and stupidity might have cost him his job. Worse than that, he might never have got another if anything had happened to the Lady or you. That's a fine thing to do to a good friend."

Fred tried to intercede. "It was partly my fault," he said. "I should never have let Sandy coax me into letting her take the Lady out alone."

"It's her fault," Bill insisted. "Every bit of it. Don't try to excuse her, because she doesn't deserve it. She took advantage of you. She planned this whole thing. Deliberately. Waiting until I wasn't around to try jumping with the Lady. She knew what she was doing. She knows enough about horses to understand the risk she was taking."

"I didn't think . . ." she started to say, but Bill cut her off.

"You didn't think! You thought all right, but you were thinking of only one thing. Yourself. Your own crazy notion that you wanted to jump with the Lady." He was unbearably scornful now, lashing her with his words. "You told me the other day that every time you take the Lady out you tell her you love her. It's a fine way to show your love. A fine way. By risking her life."

He turned his back on Sandy. "Poor Lady," he muttered. "You had about one chance in a hundred. It's sure a good thing your first name is Lucky."

14

BILL did not call for her the next evening. She waited for him in the kitchen, listening for the click of his heels on the walk and for the shrill, high-pitched whistle that was so peculiarly his own. But he did not come.

She waited a long time, hoping against hope that he would appear. She could stand another scolding from him. She could even stand to have him tell her again that she was selfish and a fool, but she could not stand this silence.

Twice she went to the telephone to call him up and both times she walked away without doing it. Then she went up to her room and closed the door. She could have gone down to the sandlot. She could have run over to Pat Manero's or Ellie Winchester's. She had some money left from her allowance and she could have gone to a movie. Yet she did none of these things. She lay face-down on her bed and grieved. Mingled in her sorrow was something more caustic than grief itself. There was remorse. Only now, in the emptiness of the first evening she had spent alone since she had met Wyoming Bill, did Sandy realize the rashness of the thing she had done in jumping the Lady.

Bill's right, she kept saying to herself. I was selfish and stupid. I endangered everything I love. The Lady. Fred. Bill.

The picture of what might have happened terrified her. She was not concerned about the physical danger to herself, even though Bill's words were still ringing in her ears, *"You might have been a whole lot more banged up than you are."*

That fact in itself was negligible. If anything had happened to the Lady! If Fred and Bill had lost their jobs. If Fred had never been able to get another position, with his handicap and all. In an anguish of self-condemnation, she rolled over and wept great racking sobs of painful remorse.

By the next afternoon she could no longer stand to live silently with the thoughts that were harassing her. She had to talk to someone. She asked to be excused from softball practice, jumped on her bike, and rode out to the estate. She found Fred clipping some bushes around the big Barton house, and dropping her bike on the grass, she helped him load the wheelbarrow with dead branches.

"Fred," she said as he sat down to rest, "I feel sick over what happened. I didn't think, Fred. I was so crazy to jump with the Lady. I know I don't deserve to be forgiven, but will you please be my friend again?"

"I've never stopped being your friend, Sandy."

"Bill won't speak to me. He snubs me in school. He doesn't call me up or come over to my house. I wish he'd bawl me out some more. Say anything he felt like saying. Call me stupid, foolish, anything. But I can't stand this silent treatment."

"Bill's hurt. I know, because Bill is very much as I was when I was a boy. Bill thinks you had a pretty close call, Sandy. You did. So did the Lady. If anything had happened to either of you, he figures he would have been partly to blame. After all, he did bring you over here the first time. He's responsible for introducing you to the Lady and me."

"Yes, but why did he have to keep blaming me in that stubborn way of his? He had to keep harping on it, even when you tried to stick up for me a little." She imitated Bill's tone and manner. "It's all Sandy's fault. All Sandy's fault."

Then she felt the tears rushing up inside her again. "I guess it was all my fault, Fred," she sobbed. "I never should have done it. It was a dreadful thing to do."

She pulled out a fistful of tissues. "All day I've been carrying these things around," she said. "Half a box of them. All day I've been on the point of bawling." She laughed and sobbed at the same time. "Every time I break down and cry, seems like I have to pick your shoulder to do it on."

"Go ahead," Fred said. "It's a pretty broad shoulder."

"Bill's never going to speak to me again. I can tell by the set of his jaw when he passes me in the halls at school. How can I ever tell him I'm sorry, if he won't even look at me?"

"If he won't let you tell him, maybe you can find some

way of showing him. Showing him might be a lot better. Talk is a pretty cheap commodity, and we often say things we don't mean or feel, Sandy."

She plucked a handful of grass and let it slip through her fingers. She was thinking about what Fred had just said. There was a lot of wisdom in his philosophy. There always was. After such an unforgivably selfish thing as she had done to Bill and Fred and the Lady, words did seem inadequate by way of making amends. She would have to find some way of showing Bill that she deserved his forgiveness.

She got up, feeling somewhat relieved.

"Thanks, Fred," she said. "I think I've found out what I came over for today."

Fred limped beside her as she walked her bike partway down the road that led to the exit gate of the estate. They were quiet now, saying little in contrast with their earlier talkativeness, but the silence between them was a warm and sympathetic one.

As she turned to say good-by, Fred put his hand on her shoulder and said, "Don't worry too much, Sandy. Everything's going to work out all right."

It was so much like him to encourage her at this moment when she most needed it. She jumped on her bike and rode off as fast as she dared before Fred could see that the tears were welling up again.

She went home determined to watch for her opportunity to show Bill that she was genuinely sorry. She had not the faintest notion when that chance would come or what she would do, but with her whole heart she waited for it.

Bill was not very helpful. He went about his own business with a grimness that held Sandy at much more than arm's length. Now that he seemed to want nothing further to do with her, she fell over him wherever she turned. She met him in the corridors at school three times as much as she formerly had. Once as she slammed the door of her locker, he was sauntering by with a group of boys, but he lowered his head to speak to a stocky boy he was walking with, and not even the flicker of an eyelash showed that he had noticed her. It was a good thing they were not in the same year at high school. She could not have stood it if she had been obliged to sit in the same classrooms with him and look across at the set of that stubborn jaw.

As it was, she gave up expecting him to walk around the side of the house after supper. His whistle became a ghost whistle, something that ran through her mind, haunting her. Once she thought she heard it and rushed to the back door to see if he was there. He wasn't.

To her distress was added the complication of embarrassment. What was she expected to do about the Starlight Dance? He had invited her to go with him, but she could not call him up and ask if the invitation still held. Even if it did, the dance would not be any fun for either of them. So she decided that Bill was giving her credit for having sense enough to know the date was off. She made no plans for it.

Four days before the Starlight Dance, New Sharon High played Greenport away from home. Sandy's team looked forward to the game with mingled excitement and tension.

Greenport played for blood, and generally it was New Sharon's that was spilled.

As often happened, the boys' baseball team was playing Greenport too. Today Sandy did not sit at the back of the bus and watch for the cars of boys to pass them. Even if she should catch sight of Bill, he would be looking the other way.

When Sandy and her teammates hopped off the bus, the Greenport girls were already on the field, warming up. Miss MacDonald called off the starting line-up. She put in Helen Ackerson, a senior whom she was trying out as pitcher, to pitch the first part of the game. Sandy would play left field. Sandy was not surprised. She knew that Miss MacDonald was disciplining her for what had happened at Westbrook.

Helen was a so-so pitcher. She was better than Pat Manero. She had a fairly good arm, and when she was not tired she pitched well, but she did not have that extra little something that lifts a pitcher out of the mediocre class.

There was some discussion about who would umpire the game. Greenport wanted to use a boy umpire and asked if Miss MacDonald would agree, letting the Greenport boy act as plate umpire and appointing a New Sharon boy as base umpire.

"If you had notified me in time," Miss MacDonald replied, "I could have brought a boy with me. How can I get a New Sharon boy now?"

Pat Manero spoke up. "The boys are playing baseball," she said. "Maybe there's someone with the team who could act as umpire." Miss MacDonald agreed, and Pat went racing over to the boys' field to return in a few minutes with—of all people—Bill!

The boy umpires took their places on the field as New Sharon got ready to bat. A bristling, grown-in crew cut made the Greenport umpire resemble an angry porcupine. He was small, and he made up for his short stature by throwing his stentorian voice halfway to New Sharon and back every time he opened his mouth.

"Batter up!" he thundered, and Sandy was glad she was not going to pitch. He's a scrapper, she thought.

The first inning was a pushover—for Greenport. Their pitcher was bad news. She was one of those scrawny, underfed girls that looked as if she had never even gripped a ball in her life, much less pitched one. She slouched up to the rubber as if she would just about make it. Still in a fog, she went into a listless windup. Then—*wham!* The ball came at the New Sharon batter like a bullet, and the trumpet-voiced umpire boomed, "Strr-i-ike!"

He made three syllables of it, dragging it out in gleeful triumph. When you heard the jubilation in his voice as he called a strike against New Sharon, you didn't have to guess very hard which school he belonged to!

When New Sharon went into the field, Helen Ackerson pitched them too high. If it hadn't been that Sandy, in the outfield, had always been good at catching fly balls, the inning might have lasted all afternoon. Sandy caught two flies, putting out two Greenport girls. The third was put out when tagged while running from second to third. But Greenport had scored four runs to New Sharon's zero before that happened.

The second inning was not much better than the first, and it ended with a score of 6–0 in favor of Greenport.

The top of the third was a nightmare for New Sharon. They made every mistake in the book and invented a few of their own. Roz Lauterbach went haywire. She was one of those players who needs to be encouraged constantly from the sidelines while she is up at bat. You had to shout, "You can do it, Roz. Sure you can," and you had to keep it up all the time she was swinging at them. At bat, she had about as much moral courage as a rabbit that has just run into the arms of a wildcat.

But today no amount of encouragement got through to her. Twice she swung at the pitches so wildly that Greenport rooters were almost rolling off the bleachers in hilarity.

"She's a comedian," they roared. "She ought to be on TV."

That did it. Roz almost collapsed on the field. She was so sure she wouldn't hit the pitches that she never did.

Pat Manero was next. Usually one of the best batters on the team, Pat was struck out by three straight strikes. One, two, three. Just like that. You would have sworn it couldn't happen to Pat, but it did.

Then Midge Dubois, the new sophomore on the New Sharon team, surprised them all. She hit the first ball that was pitched to her—hit it hard and fair, and ran to first base.

Sandy was next. As she picked up the bat, she had a

fleeting glimpse of Bill standing in the base umpire's position between first and second. He was staring hard at something behind her.

There was some heckling from the Greenport rooters, but Sandy was used to that. Greenport knew she was New Sharon's ace pitcher. The rival team always tried to upset the pitcher, whether she was on the rubber or up at bat. You had to expect that.

Her first ball was a strike. She let the next go by because she was sure it was a ball, but the umpire called it a strike. So what could she do? She grabbed the bat as if she meant business and swung at the next. It was a base-line foul. The ball went back to the pitcher. Midge, on first, left her base, thinking Sandy had been struck out, and Bill had to call Midge out.

The New Sharon girls shouted their disgust. "It was only a foul, Midge. Why did you leave your base?"

"The first baseman told me it was three strikes," she said, red-faced.

"Look," her teammates shouted in dismay, "don't believe *anything* anyone tells you in a game. That's the idea. To confuse you and get you out."

"Sandy!" Miss MacDonald was beckoning to her. "I'm putting you in as pitcher at the bottom of the third." Any other time Sandy would have flashed Miss MacDonald a look of gratitude for letting bygones be bygones, but today she would have preferred to keep her position in the outfield. She had no relish for this game. She disliked junior umpires. She was upset because Bill was out on the field, standing there, but avoiding her glance.

As she started toward the pitcher's plate, Miss MacDonald smiled some encouragement and said, "Just be careful what you say, Sandy." She nodded.

The minute she reached the pitcher's plate, she saw a danger signal. There was no rubber. The marker for boys' softball was forty-three feet from home plate to pitcher's box and it had been spiked into the ground. Therefore it was no use in a girls' game, in which the pitching distance was thirty-five feet. The pitcher was expected to stand back of a line drawn in the dirt by the umpire's toe!

Sandy wound up and let go. "Ball!" blared the umpire. She tried again, and again he called it a ball. Twice more she went into her favorite pretzel windup and twice more the umpire called, "Ball." The Greenport batter walked to first base.

Sandy decided to switch her windup and try Bill's famous windmill.

She wound up, swinging her arm up and down, up and down, and as the ball left her hand, she shifted her weight and broke contact with the imaginary pitcher's plate. It took the Greenport batter by surprise, bewildering her because she did not know on which swing of Sandy's arm the pitch would come. Sandy put the batter out in short order.

The next two girls were struck out too. This was more like it. The score at the end of the third was still 6–0 in favor of Greenport, but at least the cocky team was being held down.

Sandy's pitching gave new hope to her team. They

made three runs at the top of the fourth inning. As the Greenport team came up to bat at the bottom of the inning, there was consternation in their ranks. The tide was turning and in the opinion of the Greenport players and rooters, Sandy was to blame. She was well aware, during her warm-up, that the Greenport girls were looking at her and whispering among themselves.

She gave herself plenty of time on the pitch. The first batter up was too serious for her own good. Sandy knew how to pitch to a worried batter. Delay the pitch, use a long windup, and then a slow ball.

It worked. Sandy struck the batter out, but she saw the row of Greenport heads go into another whispering huddle. Something was bothering them. They pointed to Sandy and then to the imaginary pitcher's plate. One of the girls jumped off the wall on which most of the Greenport team was sitting and ran over to the umpire. There was a long discussion. The umpire called over to Sandy that she would have to be more careful about keeping her feet back of the line when she delivered the ball.

Sandy looked over at the Greenport players. They were nudging each other. Sandy's first impulse was anger at the umpire. She had not been stepping over the line. Greenport was only trying to rattle her. The loud voice of the umpire and the injustice of the rebuke had all the makings of a rhubarb, but she remembered two things just in time—Miss MacDonald's caution and Bill's presence behind her on the field.

"All right," she answered. "I'll watch it."

The girls were not satisfied with Sandy's docile acceptance of the rebuke. They wanted more of a rumpus. They needled the umpire and in turn he nagged Sandy. She kept her tongue under control, but her concern over where she was stepping fouled up her pitching. The umpire called one ball after another. She walked two batters, and the next made a hit that loaded the bases.

She must stop this. Control—that's what would do it. Bill had preached it to her a hundred times. "Control," he would say, "is the pitcher's most important asset. A good arm is swell. A tricky windup is fine, but it's control that wins the game."

So she forced herself to calm down. She took her time. She ignored the heckling from the bleachers. She ignored the needling about stepping over the line. She even conquered the impulse to fight back. She kept one thing in mind, the thing Bill had told her was most important of all—control. She managed to put out two more Greenport batters without permitting that team to make a single run.

At the top of the fifth, New Sharon made four runs, which put them one ahead of Greenport. Then, to add to Greenport's discomfort, Sandy struck out three girls in the bottom of the fifth when Greenport came up to bat. One, two, three, out! It was as easy as that.

When Greenport came into the field at the top of the sixth, they looked determined. The Greenport pitcher, giving everything she had, duplicated Sandy's performance in the fifth by putting out three batters in a row. New Sharon was not able to score. Then, in the last half of the sixth, in spite of Sandy's best efforts, Greenport managed to score one run, making it a 7–7 tie.

The seventh inning started off quietly enough. Too quietly. Something in Greenport's manner as they took the field—a certain smugness and overconfidence—stirred up an uneasiness in Sandy. Then she saw what had happened. They had put in a new pitcher.

This was no ordinary seventh-inning relief pitcher. She was Lefty MacCracken, a southpaw, with a formidable reputation in high-school softball. Good in all sports, she had been injured in a hockey game last fall and had been out of softball all season. Now she was able to play a little, and Greenport had been saving her for just such an emergency.

Even Sandy had respect for Lefty MacCracken. She had intelligence to back up her good pitching arm.

Lefty warmed up with the poise of a professional. She was a tall, good-looking girl with the blackest black hair Sandy had ever seen and spots of high color in her cheeks. Greenport rallied as they watched Lefty throw the ball to their catcher. She was their trump card.

Pat Manero was up first. Pat, too, had a reputation in high-school softball as one of the best batters in the league, and Lefty knew it.

Lefty wound up and delivered. "Ball!" the umpire called. He sounded so pleased that Sandy became suspicious. The second pitch was a ball, and so was the third. Then Sandy saw what Lefty was up to.

Ten to one the next will be a ball too, Sandy thought.

Sure enough. Pat was walked to first. That was nice

going for Lefty MacCracken, very clever planning. This was big-league stuff. She was smart enough to know that Pat was New Sharon's most dangerous hitter and that if she could put Pat on first base and keep Pat there while preventing the rest of the team from hitting, there would be no runs in this inning.

Midge Dubois was nervous as she came up to bat. Lefty pitched them to her slow and Midge swung at them too late. After two strikes, she made a contact and the ball rolled into the infield near first base. Midge was tagged at first and Pat, forced to second, was tagged on a double play just as she slid in.

"Two out!" the umpire bellowed.

Sandy was up next. She could feel Lefty looking her over. From Sandy's restlessness, Lefty would probably figure she was a nervous batter. Nothing was further from the truth. She was always a little excited before the first hit, but it was not due to anxiety. She knew she could hit them, and hit them hard.

Lefty was not the only one who was doing some sizing up. While Sandy had waited her turn at bat, she had been doing some analyzing of her own. Lefty MacCracken was a versatile pitcher. She had a repertory of windups that was unusual for a high-school pitcher. She had a jet-propelled fast ball and a teaser of a slow ball. Most of the girls on the softball teams were "guess batters." They did not try too hard to figure out a pitcher's technique, but just held the bat and swung when the ball came at them. With this kind of batting, a smart girl like Lefty was in the driver's seat. She could vary her balls, change her pace, and by taking the average batter by surprise, get a maximum number of strike-outs.

But Sandy was not the average batter. She was a past master at this art of deception herself, and because she had always studied her own weaknesses, she could see that Lefty had a few too.

For instance, Lefty gave away in advance the kind of pitch she was going to deliver. You only had to watch her windups. When the pitch was going to be a fast one, she used one variation of the figure-eight windup. On her slow balls, she used another variation of the same windup. The distinction was slight. You had to be a good pitcher yourself and have eyes like a hawk to detect the difference, but if you watched closely, you could see her signal the type of ball it would be every time.

Sandy got ready. Lefty's windup was beautiful. The ball came at Sandy fast and she let it go. She had figured she would not hit until she got the ball she wanted.

"Strike!" the umpire called.

Sandy made a great show of uneasiness, shuffling her feet. She was baiting Lefty, letting her believe she had been upset by the umpire. She was sure the next one would be too high or too low or have too much curve. Lefty would figure that Sandy would swing this time because a batter usually swings at the second pitch, even if it is outside the striking area, when the first pitch has been called a strike.

Lefty wound up and released. Sure enough. It had too much curve and Sandy let it go.

"Ball," the umpire called.

Sandy gripped the bat first low, then high, then low. She appeared to be unable to make up her mind. She could almost see Lefty thinking, This New Sharon pitcher is a poor batter. If I keep my pitches low and my balls fast, she won't stand a chance.

Lefty wound up and let go another fast ball, this time well within the striking area and just low enough, so she thought, to make it a hard one for Sandy to bat.

Sandy swung, deliberately too high. She would wait for the next ball. It would be faster than the others. It would be low, but it would have that touch of overconfidence that Sandy knew about all too well. That would be the pitch Sandy was waiting for.

"Two strikes!" the Greenport umpire called in apparent satisfaction.

Lefty drew herself up, a fine figure of a girl in complete control of the situation. She was good, and she knew it. She knew it, perhaps, just a touch too well.

She crouched low now, for her special fast-ball windup, and released the ball. It came at Sandy fast and low.

This is it, she thought. This is my ball.

She met it head on, in just the right spot and with every bit of weight she could pack behind it. She dropped the bat and ran, letting her legs fly. First base. Be sure to touch them all. Touch them clean and fair so Bill can see you do it. Second base. Third base.

She was conscious of nothing but her flying legs, her breath coming hard, and the dust flying up around her. She was down on her sandlot where she had begun, running her legs off to make it a homer.

There was shouting. Wild screams—piercing, deafening. It would have bothered her if she had been conscious of it. She wasn't. All she wanted to do was to touch home plate.

She did. She did it a split second before the ball reached the catcher's mitt.

"A homer!" someone screamed, jumping up and down. "Sandy, you made a homer!" It was a moment or two before the significance of this particular scream sank in. Then Sandy saw that it was Dodo shouting in her ear. Dodo, the imperturable.

The last half of the seventh inning was one of those shambles that develops when a strong team knows it is beaten and won't admit it. Lefty MacCracken had been Greenport's master stroke. They had tried her and failed. The score was now 8–7 in favor of New Sharon.

Greenport began to take a lot of unnecessary precautions. They changed their base coaches. They complained about the condition and quality of the softballs. They looked over the bats and found two with cracks and insisted that they be discarded. They requested the umpire to deliver a lecture to Sandy on where to stand and how to pitch. He made a great show of instructing her, marking off the line with grandiose precision, and saying that if she did not keep her feet back of it when she released the ball, he would have to do something more drastic than give warnings.

"You've been getting away with too much in this game," he said.

Sandy wanted to retort, "You mean that homer I just

scored?" but she kept quiet and warmed up for a knockout blow to Greenport.

She was so angry that she hurled three pitches over to strike the first batter out.

Greenport sent up a howl. "Keep your feet back of the pitching line!" the rooters shouted.

Sandy was not moved. She knew she was not stepping over the line. The next batter up was a hard-hitting girl who walloped the ball into the infield and reached first base. Another stepped up to bat.

Sandy wound up and let go a fast pitch that went right over the plate. It was a strike. Sandy delivered another fast one and again the umpire called, "Strike!"

The girl on first had her foot at the edge of the bag, tapping her toe impatiently. She expected the next to be a hit, and she was ready to run to second.

Sandy swung her arm up and down, using Bill's windmill technique and releasing the ball after a long windup. From the corner of her eye, she saw the girl on first move just before she released the ball. She wondered if Bill had seen it too. The batter swung and the umpire called, "Foul."

Bill spoke up. "Girl on first is out!" he shouted.

"Why?" questioned the Greenport girl who was coaching first base.

"She stepped off the bag before the ball left the pitcher's hands."

"I didn't see her do that."

Bill didn't answer. He called over to the plate umpire, "Girl on first goes out. That's two outs."

The Greenport umpire turned to the scorer as if undecided what to do, but before he had a chance to say anything, the Greenport girl coaching first base ran over to him. There was some talk and the umpire shouted to Bill, "She says you're wrong. The girl didn't leave first base until the pitcher released the ball."

Bill walked over. "First base is my territory," he said. "My decision is supposed to hold."

"Not if someone says it isn't correct."

Bill's jaw tightened. "I happen to be telling the truth," he said quietly. "The girl left first base."

"I can't call the girl on first out unless you've got proof."

"You don't have to call her out," Bill replied in the same quiet tone of finality. "I called her out. That settles it."

Pat Manero, who was playing first base for New Sharon today, came into the discussion. "If you want proof," she said, "I can give it. I saw that girl step off first base before the ball left Sandy's hands."

"You're from the same school," the Greenport umpire said. "You'd naturally stick together."

Sandy couldn't keep out of the argument any longer. "I saw the girl on first step off too soon," she said.

The Greenport umpire wheeled on her. "You'd better stay out of this," he said. "Greenport's already lost plenty because you didn't stay back of the line when you delivered the ball."

Sandy kept her anger under control but she asked, "What has that got to do with this play?"

"You keep out of this, I said," the umpire told her. He

gave her a shove. Sandy almost lost her balance and just saved herself from sprawling in the dust.

Bill grabbed him by the shoulder and swung him around, pulling the boy's sweater into a tight knot at the chest. "Don't speak to Sandy Herzog like that," he said.

"Why not?"

"Because I've watched this game and I've let your decisions go unchallenged even when I didn't agree with them. I kept quiet because I figured it was none of my business. I knew I didn't have any right to protest your judgment." Bill tightened his hold. "But now you've started this rhubarb and I feel I've got a right to speak up. Go back to your place and let our pitcher alone. Don't put your hands on her again." Bill let go of him.

The umpire turned and walked back to his position behind home plate, his cockiness gone. The argument broke up and the two coaches relaxed as the New Sharon girls took their places on the field.

Before she walked back to her catcher's position, Dodo stopped to talk to Sandy.

"Are you all right, Sandy?" she asked. "All you've got to do now is put one more batter out and the game is ours. It's an important pitch but I know you can do it. You're all right, aren't you?"

"I never felt better in my life," Sandy answered, as her eyes found Bill's and he smiled at her.

She went back to take her place behind that narrow line drawn in the dust by the umpire's foot and struck the next batter out on three straight strikes.

15

SANDY waited in the kitchen for Bill to pick her up for the dance. She watched for him by the screen door, standing up because it seemed quite impossible to sit down in her new dress, and she listened, not too patiently, for Bill's whistle.

Bill was prompt. The wall clock indicated one minute before seven-thirty as Bill's whistle rounded the corner of the house. When, looking handsome in a new dark blue suit, he threw open the screen door and saw Sandy, his whistle stopped short.

His eyes told her first what he was thinking, then his smile, and finally he said, "Sandy, you're a knockout in that dress. It's terrific."

The dress was a gift from Fred, who had wanted to give Sandy something for posing for him and decided a dress for the Starlight Dance was the pleasantest way he could show his gratitude. It was a yellow dress, and Bill said it reminded him of a spring morning "out home," of bright sunshine on waving yellow grasses.

"I'm glad you're my girl, Sandy," he said.

They drove out to show Fred the dress before they went on to the dance. He was waiting for them at the side door of his cottage and Sandy had to turn around several times while he admired her from every angle.

"Now we'll have to start painting you all over again," he said. He was thoughtful a moment and then added, "Bill, I hope we're not spoiling our girl. She may get so fond of being all dressed up that she won't want to get into her frontier pants and shirt and ride the Lady any more."

"Not me!" Sandy spoke with vehemence. "I'd never change about that." Only then did she catch the twinkle that passed from Fred to Bill.

Sandy enjoyed the dance more than she had dreamed possible. She exchanged dances with every girl on the softball team and, to her surprise, she found that dancing and conversing with so many different kinds of boys was an interesting experience.

When the dance was over, she and Bill were invited to join some of the couples who were going out to the Red Galleon for sandwiches. Here they danced some more in the small floor space cleared away between the tables. Sandy found herself suddenly popular, but this was not the same kind of popularity she had experienced at Elsie Sherman's square-dance party. This was something strangely exciting. The boys flocked around her and they were all attentive and lavish with their compliments. They liked her new yellow dress. The color and style were perfect, they said. They admired the way she was wearing her hair. It left her breathless and a little bewildered, but happier than she had ever been before, happier even than the day they had beaten Greenport, more excited than if she had knocked out three home runs in one game.

One of the boys, a boy she had never even seen before tonight, asked her for a date. He was from Brighthaven and had come to the dance with Wendy Mason's sister. He moved his chair up to the table where Sandy was sitting and asked her for a date right in front of Bill.

"You're a lot of fun, Sandy," the boy said. "If I bring my brother over next Friday, will you get another girl and go on a double date?"

Sandy was so surprised that she burst out, "Well, I should say not! I've got a date with a horse named Lucky Lady next Friday."

Bill was still laughing at Sandy's retort when he turned the Peabody car down Gardner Street and parked in front of the sandlot.

He pulled Sandy toward him. "Sandy, why didn't you accept that boy's invitation? He seemed like a decent chap. Nice-looking. Pleasant. I wouldn't have minded."

"You wouldn't have minded!"

"I wouldn't have the right to mind," Bill replied. "You're an attractive girl. We've got to expect these things to happen. Lucky Lady and Fred and I can't keep you all to ourselves."

"I'm not so sure I like your generosity," she answered. "I would have minded very much if you had accepted such an invitation from a Brighthaven girl. Brighthaven! Of all places!"

"Sandy, a boy who had you for a girl wouldn't want

to go out with anyone else. Can't you see that? That's why all the boys took to you tonight. You've got that something extra."

"What do you mean, that something extra?"

"I can't explain it, Sandy. You either have it or you don't. And you've got it, whether you're pitching softball or riding the Lady or doing the Charleston. I guess it's just because you're you. It's like that boy said tonight, you're a lot of fun."

"Then even if you go back to Wyoming, maybe you won't forget all the good times we've had together."

"I could never forget the good times, or you either." He leaned down and kissed her.

"Wyoming must be wonderful," she said. "I'd love to go out there. I'd love to see it just once."

"We can almost always get what we want if it's right for us to have it and if we hope hard enough."

"Do you think I ever will see Wyoming, Bill? Do you honestly think so?"

"Sure you will. We've got an old waddy named Sam on our ranch. Whenever he's convinced something is bound to happen, he always says, 'I feel it in my horse's bones.' That's the way I feel about your coming out home, Sandy. I feel it in Lucky Lady's bones."

Sandy sat up, full of anticipation over the pleasure that Bill was so sure lay ahead of her one of these days. "I want to see everything, Bill, just the way you've described it. The ranch and the waddies and the shining mountains and the cottonwood trees blowing their white tufts on the river, and the grass—especially the grass all bright and golden and full of color. I want to see it all. I want to meet your sister too." Then, after a quiet moment, "Do you think your mother will like me? I don't remember my own mother and it's very important to have your mother like me, Bill."

"My mother likes you already."

"Why, she doesn't even know me!"

"She knows you all right. I've taken care of that." Bill pulled a folded paper from his pocket. "I wrote my mother about you the other day." He held out the paper to her. "This is a copy of my letter. I made it for you, because these are the things I think about you and I want you to know them, Sandy."

She unfolded the sheet of paper and while Bill held a flashlight for her, she read what he had written.

"There's a girl here I want to tell you about, Mother. I met her on a sandlot on the street where we both live. Right from the start I took to her because she's so natural and genuine. We have a lot in common. She plays a good game of softball. She loves horses. She likes people too, and people like her a lot. She's the kind of girl you can feel comfortable with.

"I've been spending most of my time with her because she's so much fun. But more than that, she's the kind of girl who will grow along with me. You know what I mean. There are some people we meet and we like them for a while, but then they go one way and we go another. Sandy's a girl who will grow right along with a fellow, so instead of going different ways, I'm sure we'll be going the same way for a long, long time.

"I want you to know, Mother, how much I respect and admire and love my *Sandlot Sandy,* because one of these days I know you'll both meet each other."

She folded the paper and put it in the little clutch bag that had once been Marlene's but now was hers. She did not spoil this moment by talking. She sat quietly, feeling choked up, as if it were too much to have happen all at once.

She looked out across the sandlot, gray and eerie in the half-light cast by the moon.

My sandlot, she thought. The place they nicknamed me after. In a rush of memory, she recalled all the things that had happened to her here. The early games of softball when she had learned to pitch so well. The afternoons spent coaching the Blue Devils and the Supermen. The long summer evenings of square dancing and playing games and eating ice-cream cones and yelling your head off until it was bedtime. She had met Bill here, and tonight he had told her in his own way that he was very, very fond of her.

All the important things that have ever happened to me, she thought, have happened right here.

Then, turning her face up toward Bill's, she said, "I remember something you once told me, Bill. It was at Elsie Sherman's party."

"What was it?"

"You said, *'Sandy, never underestimate the power of a sandlot.'* " She smiled and put her hand into his. "After tonight, Bill, I'm sure I never could."